ETHEREAL MALIGNANCE

THE ETHEREAL INFESTANCE

BOOK ONE

D.P. VAUGHAN

D.P. VAUGHAN

ETHEREAL MALIGNANCE

CHAPTER ONE

The late afternoon sun bathed the neighbourhood in orange, but John Wedgewood preferred the shadows and the dark. He stood out as a solitary figure in the sunlit leafy street, but in the shade, he was a moving shadow. People wouldn't mess with you if they didn't notice you.

The occasional fallen branch lay on the path from yesterday's storm, and the sunlight was punctuated at regular intervals by the shade of houses and trees.

John wore black full-length cargo pants, black runners, and a black T-shirt largely covered by a black leather jacket—the most valuable thing he owned. His dark skin complemented his black hair, coarse, short and tight curls fading down the sides. The nineteen-year-old's shoulders were hunched, and he moved with purpose.

John walked through the neighbourhood, a patchwork of manicured lawns and sprawling large houses. As he passed, curtains twitched, and faces peered at him, their expressions tight and disapproving. A man watering his lawn turned the hose off and watched him until he was out of sight. The message was clear. It may have been 1993, but to John, it felt like just another day of survival.

His only friend, Griffin, lived a handful of blocks away. His shack was hidden behind a thick row of trees in the park. Griffin Tree Row, he called it, often joking that he'd lived there longer than the trees. Back then, John had visited Griffin after classes and sometimes instead of. Since he'd dropped out of high school, he visited him on a near-daily basis. Griffin: the strange old man who lived in the park.

John often thought about how good it would be to leave the city. Head into the woods and never deal with other people and their bullshit ever again. He didn't let the fact he had no survival skills dampen his fantasy. He would be free. If he ever won the lottery, that's what he would do. Of course, you had to actually buy lottery tickets to win, and John didn't have the money for that sort of thing. He strode on, deep in his inner dream world.

Meanspirited laughter cut through the street. John froze. There was trouble a block away: a group of school bullies who had since graduated to full-time delinquency. They were led by Tom, the brains of the bunch if you defined "brains" loosely. They were only seventeen but had dropped out of school younger than even John had. It was only a matter of time before they were in jail. People said the same about him, but these idiots went out of their way to cause trouble. John kept to himself and tried to avoid the trouble the world made for him.

If he'd done even a small amount of what these idiots had, the police would have taken him away a long time ago. It was obvious that the difference in the way he and they were treated was skin deep. However, even they could only get away with so much, and then they'd be off the streets.

John frowned.

Strange. They normally lurked about the bike racks in the early morning, harassing schoolkids.

They must have stayed back for a particular reason. Or

person. It wouldn't have been for John because he didn't have a schedule for anything except smoking.

He considered his options and took a draw of his cigarette. Cutting through the yard of the house nearby would take him to the next street over, and then he could jump the fence to get back on track a few blocks later. John had no intention of getting his arse beaten.

Someone cried out for help: a pudgy kid he didn't know, still in school uniform. They had him surrounded. One of the bullies punched him, and he went down like a sack of bricks.

John's fists balled up, his heart drumming a rapid rhythm in his chest. His jaw set, teeth gritting, eyes homing in on the unfolding scene. A familiar heat kindled in his gut, a flame stoked by memories of his own childhood. He remembered the sting of fists, the taste of blood, the laughter of those who thought power meant hurting the weak. Bullies always liked to punch down; he knew that from his childhood. The smart choice wasn't so appealing now. If he could distract the vicious idiots long enough for the kid to get away, he could bolt through the yards and jump the fences. If he were lucky, they'd get bored chasing him before too long. He took a deep breath and stepped forward.

"What's up, dickheads?" John called out. He smoked his cigarette in an attempt to look unfazed and nonchalant.

They looked over, their expressions shifting in a way John interpreted as surprise. They probably weren't used to people daring to interfere with their fun or deliberately drawing their attention.

John blew smoke into the air.

"You boys must be so brave, taking on one kid all by yourselves."

Tom sneered. His facial features and crewcut made him look more rat-like than John remembered. "What, is this your boyfriend, orphan?" He punctuated the question with a kick to the downed victim's ribs. The kid sobbed and looked up at John pleadingly.

Two of the group headed towards him, but John needed them all for the kid to have a chance of escape. He flicked his lit cigarette towards the bullies. "Why? Jealous?"

That did it. They stalked towards John, the beaten-up kid forgotten but staying down.

"Run, you idiot. Run!"

The kid jumped to his feet and awkwardly limped away.

John grinned nervously at the bullies and made a break for it, his feet pounding the pavement as he sprinted away, the bullies' shouts and thunder of their footsteps close behind.

An impact hit him from the side. He hit the ground, winded, not expecting the tackle. They rolled him onto his back. *Shit.* He couldn't breathe in. Only out. *Shit, shit, shit.*

Bright spots accompanied the pain as the first punch landed against his head. He threw his hands up in defence, but it was pointless. They all piled on, punching and kicking.

One of the lackeys grabbed John from behind and dragged him to his feet to face Tom. He stared back in defiance despite his injuries, and breathed loudly through gritted teeth.

"Not so fucking tough now, are you?" Tom said before punching him in the gut.

John tried to double over in pain but was held in place.

He copped a fist right in the eyebrow which split and oozed blood. Another caught him in the cheek and mouth, splitting his lip. Then the nose, which miraculously didn't break. John couldn't move, couldn't fight back. He coughed blood onto Tom's face in defiance.

Tom's eyes widened for a moment, then narrowed into dangerous slits. His nostrils flared, his breathing harsh and ragged, and his face turned an ugly shade of red. He raised his fist, knuckles white with the intensity of his grip.

John shut his eyes and tried to turn his head, waiting for the inevitable blow. He'd gambled and lost.

"This looks to be a fun game. Care if I join in?" came a lilting, droll voice.

Through bleary and bloodied eyes John recognised the familiar figure of an exceptionally old, bald man.

"No, Griffin! They'll kill you!" John said, but a backhand to the face sent him reeling to the ground. He spat blood onto the dirt. "He's just an old man. Leave him—"

A kick to the ribs silenced him. He grabbed his side and gasped for breath.

Battered, bloodied, and bruised, he squinted at the scene unfolding before him. His stomach fell and tears welled. He couldn't breathe. Couldn't get up. He couldn't save him.

It's all my fault.

"You should watch where you walk, old man," Tom threatened.

The gang approached him. Their skin tone ranged from sun-tanned to pale, but they were all shadows compared to the eerily luminous paleness of the short figure.

Griffin didn't respond. He merely stood still and waited, the image of patience. He had no hair—not even eyelashes or eyebrows—and pale skin where fingernails should be. The youths stopped shy, seemingly creeped out by his appearance and his lack of fear. They looked to Tom for guidance. He gave a curt nod.

Rick, the dumbest of the bunch, threw a punch and John clenched his eyes shut. He couldn't watch, especially when it was his own fault. But the noise of pain didn't come from Griffin. He looked up.

Griffin held Rick's fist.

Rick squawked in pain, knees buckling before the old man who stared down at him with an amused curve to his lips.

The wet cracks of breaking bones was nauseating. Rick shrieked a high-pitched wail.

Griffin let him go and he fell to the ground, sobbing and cradling his ruined hand.

"You might want to seek medical attention for that," Griffin said.

Tom's group eyed each other warily.

He must have decided leadership was needed because he drew a knife. Griffin didn't move other than to cock his head to the side with cold bemusement. Tom darted forward and shoved his blade deep into the old man's gut.

John almost vomited.

Griffin remained still like a statue. The other bullies exchanged glances, their faces a mix of shock and confusion, their bravado faltering. But when Griffin finally moved, it wasn't for the knife. He grabbed Tom by the throat and squeezed. The rat-faced bully choked and gagged, his eyes bulging. The others stepped back, their faces pallid, their eyes wide with fear.

"Not what you expected, is it?" Griffin said with a vicious grin.

He squeezed harder. More choking sounds. Tom's limbs flailed about uselessly. No one else moved.

John pushed himself to a seated position, unable to stop staring at the knife hilt sticking out of Griffin's gut.

Griffin threw Tom to the dirt where he writhed and grasped at his throat, coughing and spluttering. He pathetically shuffled away like a wounded animal.

With a hard yank, Griffin pulled the knife out and regarded it for a moment.

"Here, you forgot this," he said and threw it at Tom, its hilt smashing into his face.

Tom clutched at his nose and blood streamed around his fingers.

"Oh, dear. That's a broken nose all right. Looks like it's off to the hospital with you, too."

John stared, wide-eyed, as his friend ambled towards him. Griffin put out his hand and pulled him to his feet. He stood unsteadily. His eyebrow and bottom lip stung and bled.

Griffin turned to the bullies. "Well, this was fun, but if you gentlemen don't mind, my friend and I are going to depart."

They dispersed in a flurried panic as if threatened with violence.

Griffin chuckled drolly. His aged clothes were torn but there wasn't any blood that John could see.

How is he even standing?

Griffin slapped him twice on the shoulder. "Let's go. And make it quick. It's my last sunset and I don't want to miss it."

Chapter Two

John's eyes darted from Griffin's face to where he'd been stabbed and back again. He swallowed hard, throat dry. "The knife ... Are you hurt?"

Griffin was helping him to his shack, and he shook his head and smiled. "If time itself hasn't killed me yet, those idiots certainly wouldn't be able to." His face was so pale blue veins were visible through the skin.

John was too exhausted to question it further.

They passed a bicycle still secured to the bike rack, and he idly wondered if it belonged to the kid. They walked from the street into the green of the trees and grass of the park. John adjusted his stride to avoid a downed tree branch.

It hurt to breathe, but he insisted on clearing the air.

"I was an idiot for getting you into that situation."

Griffin was the only person whose opinion John cared about. He was worried he'd think less of him for not only putting him at risk but also partaking in violence like the other bullies.

"Nonsense, dear boy. Your bravery is commendable." Griffin stopped and looked at him carefully for a moment. "But the next time you fight, make sure you can win."

John smiled slightly, then winced as his split lip reopened.

"When I was a younger man," Griffin said, "back in the old land, men would fight duels to the death. A bit of fisticuffs is tame fare in comparison."

John frowned and instantly regretted it as his eyebrow throbbed. "I didn't know that sort of thing was so recent."

Griffin looked to the ground for a few moments before he responded.

"Well, I'm afraid I haven't been entirely honest with you about a few things, my boy."

John's attention zeroed in on Griffin, his injuries forgotten for the moment, and a yawning chasm of fear grew in his chest. Surely the one person who treated him like a real person hadn't lied to him all these years.

"What do you mean?"

"I'm actually quite a bit older than you think. Older than anyone ought to be, really."

"I don't know," John said with a slight smile, "you seem pretty old."

Griffin laughed. A welcome sound that made John feel at home.

"I mean, more like a century longer than you think."

John relaxed. "Right," he replied with a smirk.

"I'm serious, John," Griffin said, stopping in his tracks. "All those 'Tales from the old land' I used to tell you? They weren't stories. No one back home has ever heard them. You're the only living person who has."

"I don't understand," John said. "The stories of monsters and body-snatchers? You're saying they're, what, real?"

Griffin avoided his eyes. "Yes, but replace those terms with 'ethereal beings,' and you're more on the right track."

John eyed Griffin carefully. His friend must have lost his mind with old age. Or it was some elaborate joke he wasn't going to fall for.

"Ethereal beings?"

"Yes. There are light ones and dark ones, but don't misunderstand: they're all malevolent. They just shine brightly or darkly, if that makes sense."

It doesn't.

"Light and dark ones? Like, racially?" John asked, confused.

Griffin shook his head. "Oh, no, nothing like that. Light like a blinding spotlight and dark like a gaping void."

"Uh … huh," John said.

"They're both otherworldly creatures, but the main difference appears to be how they go about things. The light creatures are much more subtle and less obvious, whereas the dark creatures are more blunt and obvious in their malevolence."

"So, there's a good side and a bad side?" John asked.

"Not at all. The light creatures are just as bad."

John rubbed his forehead. He had no idea what to say.

Griffin nodded soberly. "They're a malignance in the world. An … *infestance*, if you will."

John leaned towards Griffin.

"Infestance? I know I missed a lot of school, but I don't think that's a word."

Griffin smiled at him wryly. "I've been speaking this language since before your country was even born, so allow an old man some creative indulgences? And besides"—he winked at John— "the purpose of language is to communicate meaning, and you understood exactly what I meant, didn't you?"

"True," John conceded.

Griffin's expression turned sombre. "I discovered long ago that these creatures were in our world and took it upon myself to investigate. It wasn't long before I realised they were bad news. I've been keeping tabs on them to keep the world safe. I directly intervene when I have to, but, for the most part, I've just been trying to work out what they're after and how to stop them. I moved here because I sensed they were being drawn to this place. I wasn't sure why, and I wasn't sure exactly where, but I followed them across the sea and spent years piecing together evidence and evading their attention."

John was worried. "We need to get you to a doctor."

"Pah!" Griffin snorted. "I'll prove it!"

Griffin pushed his fist against John's hand. The gold ring on his middle finger felt cold against John's skin, and he flinched, but Griffin held his arm still.

"Wait."

John's eyebrow and lip itched for a moment, then stopped. He touched his face. He couldn't feel the wounds. His many bruises didn't hurt either, as if they'd been healed. No, that wasn't it … As if he'd never been injured in the first place.

"What …" John couldn't find the words.

"This is an anchor," Griffin said, pointing to his ring, "that the light creatures use to cling to our world. They 'take over' dead bodies and use anchors to secure themselves in our world. Otherwise, they'd lose control over the bodies and slip back into their own world. I think the healing ability is a side effect that happens when we come into contact with it."

John's shoulders weren't hunched anymore, and he stood straighter. He felt stronger than ever.

"The dark creatures have a different approach, though," Griffin said. "They don't use rings or anchors to keep themselves rooted in our world. They hunt down people and, uh … use them for fuel. This is what I meant when I said they're less subtle. A light creature can remain in a body indefinitely, but the dark creatures must hunt to recharge."

John looked horrified. "They sound like predators or parasites."

"Quite," Griffin said.

Silence fell between them.

John's mind strained as he tried to process what he'd just heard. It was insane, the stuff of horror movies, like people were cattle to these creatures. But then, Griffin had just healed him with a touch, something that was equally unbelievable. A cold dread settled in his stomach.

John looked at Griffin, his mind a whirl of conflicting emotions. Disbelief, confusion, doubt. If Griffin was right, if these creatures really existed, then the world was far more complex and terrifying than he'd ever imagined. He was standing on the edge of a precipice, staring into the unknown. And yet, he couldn't deny the evidence. His wounds were healed, and Griffin was the one who had healed them.

John took a deep breath to steady his racing heart. "Assuming you're right, of course," he said quietly, more to himself than to Griffin, his voice far more calm and composed than he felt.

No one spoke for a while.

"My apologies, John," Griffin said sombrely.

"For what?"

"For this."

Griffin let go of John and stepped back.

John blinked, confused, as searing pain blossomed across his body. His eyebrow and lip tore open like a zipper. His head became cloudy, and pain wracked his body as his bruises ached once more. His shoulders hunched, and he doubled over in pain.

"Now you know why I've lived for so long. It wasn't diet and exercise."

Griffin gently patted him on the shoulder and continued through the park towards his shack.

John jogged to catch up.

Griffin reached the shack but made no indication of heading inside. The shack was a haphazard assembly of rusted corrugated iron that had somehow stood fast against the decay of time. It was tucked away from the rest of the neighbourhood, hidden behind Griffin's Tree Row. The iron had weathered to a dull, mottled brown, streaked with patches of rust that glowed orange in the late afternoon sunlight. The structure was lopsided, leaning slightly to one side as if bowed by the weight of the years. It had no windows, just a single door that creaked and no modern amenities. It was a stark contrast to the manicured lawns and pristine houses of the neighbourhood, but it was Griffin's home.

John reached Griffin's side, next to the shack. "You say monsters are real."

"Ethereal creatures, but yes," Griffin said.

"Fine, 'ethereals' are real. And you've been tracking them all this time?"

"For about two centuries."

"Then why are you telling me this now?"

"Well, that's the thing." Griffin looked at John sadly. "I'm afraid I'm not cut out for what needs to be done anymore."

John regarded him with suspicion. "I don't understand. You're two hundred years old!"

Griffin scratched his hairless chin.

"Two hundred and twenty-six, actually."

"Not the point! You took a knife to the gut like it was nothing! Why can't you do what you need to do?"

Griffin paused a few moments.

"I've been studying these creatures for a very long time. Tracking their movements, learning their intentions, and guessing their motives. They tunnel into our reality from somewhere else"—he waved his hands about vaguely in the air— "and it's clear that they're searching for something. Well, someone, really. And they're close."

"How do you know this?"

"I've felt it. It's like a calling or a signal from a siren of old. I thought I could hold on long enough to prevent the creatures from getting to them. The feeling's been getting stronger, but I overestimated how long it would take them."

For the first time, Griffin looked exhausted.

"I'm too tired," he continued. "I lack the hunger to fight and win. After living for so long, I think one ceases to be classed as mortal. I feel like my humanity is barely holding on. If it hadn't been for your friendship, I would have lost interest in the world far sooner. I'm burned out and not strong enough to be the defender I need to be." He smiled fondly at John. "But you can."

John reeled, a knot twisting in his stomach. "How am I supposed to do it if you can't?"

"You're young and stubborn. Hell, you just got the shit beaten out of you in a fight you had no chance of winning, so you've clearly got a fire and spark inside. And if the ethereal creatures get hold of this siren of a person, I'm afraid it'll be the end of the world."

Griffin's words echoed in John's mind. He stared at the ground, his brow furrowed, as he considered the implications. The silence stretched out between them, filled only by the distant sounds of the late afternoon.

Finally, John looked up at Griffin, his eyes filled with fear and determination. "You're saying you want me to save the world?"

"Pretty much, yes."

They stared at each other with sombre expressions for several seconds.

Griffin grinned impishly. "So, no pressure, hey?"

Chapter Three

"If you don't care enough to save the world, why do you think I would? I don't care about the world or anyone. It sucks. Everyone hates me except you."

"Is that so?" Griffin asked kindly. "You picked a fight with those idiots for what? Fun?"

John shifted uncomfortably. "They're dickheads. That's all."

"Uh-huh," Griffin said.

"It's true!"

"So, you aren't curious about this ring? Wouldn't it be nice to not hurt so much?"

John hesitated. "There's a catch, though, right?"

Griffin sighed. "There's always a catch. But I find a certain poetry to using the light creatures' own anchors against them. And while the dark ones don't use anchors, they *are* vulnerable to them. This ring will literally burn them."

John looked at the golden ring on Griffin's middle finger. It looked normal, like a wedding ring. Innocuous.

Griffin looked at what could be seen of the sunset through the trees and nearby mountain to the west.

"I don't have enough time to tell you everything I should, John," Griffin said softly. "And I'm sorry to dump this burden on you."

"But—"

Griffin tore his eyes from the sunset and looked at John.

"Please," he said, "your life may depend on this. Don't underestimate these ethereal creatures. They're not human. If you vocalise any sound, they'll understand your intention."

"What, they can read minds?" John asked.

"No, not exactly. They've been here long enough to understand English, but it's more like they understand your meaning, not your words, no matter what language you use. They'll understand a cough if you have a thought behind it."

"That's weird," John said.

"Oh, you have no idea," Griffin said, raising the bare skin where eyebrows should have been. "But getting back to the point, don't underestimate them. They are relentless and will find their target wherever they go."

"What the hell can I do, then?"

Griffin smiled thinly. "I've discovered their weakness."

John raised his eyebrows, instantly regretting the pain. "Ow. What do you mean?"

"The metal in the ring led me to the solution. If the ethereal creatures can use metals like gold as anchors, then maybe other metals could do other things."

"Make sense," John said. "What did you find?"

"Lead."

"Seriously?"

"Much like blocking X-rays, I believe lead can be used to hide the person they're targeting."

"How do you know this?" John asked.

"I've been testing it for decades now."

"How?"

Griffin jerked his head in the direction of his shack. "The walls."

John baulked. "You what now?"

"The walls are lined with lead. The creatures haven't found me, so I know it works."

"Lead? Like 'lead poisoning' lead? That's what you've got in your walls?"

"Yes," Griffin said simply.

John rubbed his forehead. He'd visited the shack since his earliest days of schooling. "Have I been exposed to lead my entire life, then?"

"Well, yes and no."

John buried his head in his hands, ignoring the searing pain.

"Even if you have been exposed, putting the ring on will fix it."

John stared at him, bleary-eyed. "Uh-huh," he said flatly.

"It healed your cuts earlier, didn't it?"

"That's a good point," John said. "Wait, where the hell did *you* find so much lead?"

"Ah." Griffin shifted awkwardly. "The lead mine on the mountain. It, ah, shut down due to an accident, so I simply broke in and took what I needed."

"What lead mine?" John asked.

"The old lead mine up the mountain. Right turn at the cemetery."

"I didn't even know there was one."

"They shut it down about sixty years ago." Griffin rubbed the back of his head. "It was deemed unsafe for workers, and the monetary incentive wasn't enough to render it safe, so they just shut it down and boarded it up."

"Okay," John said, "let me get this straight. Monsters want to catch someone."

"Ethereal creatures, yes."

"And it'll be the end of the world if I don't stop them?"

Griffin nodded.

"And your solution is to find this person before they do and bring them back to your shack. Have I got everything?"

"Nowhere near everything, but you have the gist of it."

"How the hell am I supposed to find this person? Do you have an address? Or a phone number?"

"I don't know who they are."

John blinked. "You what?"

"I don't actually know who they're after."

John massaged his forehead, trying to sooth a sudden headache. "Then how—"

Griffin pointed to the south-east. "They're somewhere in that direction. Don't worry. You'll feel it when you put the ring on."

"Why haven't you done anything about it yet?" John asked. "Why?"

Griffin looked at John for a few moments. "I mentioned that for the longest time, I could sense a draw to this general area. But it was only that, a general feeling. Today is the first time that feeling has been strong enough, concentrated enough, to pinpoint a location. I don't know why, and I don't know how, but this person now shines like a beacon. They're in that direction, and they're not very far away. That's why we need to act: the ethereal creatures will have also felt this, and they'll get there first if you don't hurry."

John stared at the ground, then looked back at Griffin's pale face. "You're expecting me to take a lot on faith alone, you realise?"

Griffin nodded seriously. "I know. All I ask is that you trust me."

John sighed. Who was he to argue with the only person who'd treated him like a person and not merely a problem to be attacked or ignored?

"I trust you. I'll do it."

"Thank you," Griffin said with sincerity.

John looked away. He didn't know how to handle the appreciation.

"Oh! You'll probably need this." Griffin rummaged through his pockets and held out a twenty-dollar note expectantly.

John tilted his head.

"You know, for taxis or whatnot."

"Oh, of course," John said. He felt sheepish and took the offered money. "Thank you."

Griffin nodded silently and looked west towards the mountain. John followed his gaze. They both stared as the orange glow of sunset faded into a darkening blue. John zipped his jacket up as the twilight air made him shiver.

"You know, John," Griffin said quietly, "I can't remember the last time I was sick or hurt."

"That's a good thing, right?"

"Yes, but there's always a catch."

Griffin carefully slid the ring off his finger and held it to his face. He smiled at John and placed it in his hand.

Although he'd done it minutes earlier, the sensation was still unbelievable. The pain left his body and he felt powerful.

They stood together, the ring between their hands, for several seconds. It felt strangely formal, like a wedding ceremony or swearing an oath.

"I have faith, John, that you'll do what needs to be done."

"Thank you," John replied. "I won't let you down. I'll be back before you know it."

"I know you will."

He let go of the ring and took two steps back.

"I guess I'll be off, then?" John said.

Griffin smiled painfully, his eyes welling up, as a blast ripped through the air, shredding him to dust.

John covered his face with his forearm and clutched the ring.

Some of the dust blew onto him. He tried to brush it off and clear his face.

Griffin was gone. In his place was a cloud of rising steam and shreds of old cloth which fell like rain.

The bonds holding his ancient body together had been severed, and the man known as Griffin Pembroke was no more.

Chapter Four

John didn't move for some time.

He stood dumbstruck next to Griffin's shack, clenching the ring in his fist.

It was a trick. An elaborate prank.

The minutes passed, and nothing interrupted the chirping birds and wind rustling the trees.

No, it was real.

The ring had kept his friend alive, like a life support system. For centuries. And once he'd been disconnected from it, he was gone.

Worse, he gave up his life so John could have the ring. No, the anchor. John couldn't fully believe the idea of ethereal monsters, but his friend's departure showed a strange unnaturalness that could not be denied.

His many aches and pains had left but were replaced by an emptiness in his chest. His oldest friend and mentor was gone. John felt lonely and exposed in the darkness of the park at night. He usually preferred the dark, but right now, all he wanted was to turn the clock back to when the sun still shone, and his friend still lived.

John tried to slide Griffin's ring onto his middle finger of his right hand, but it didn't fit. He tried his ring finger, and it was tight, but at least it wouldn't fall off easily. He clenched his fist as he tried to hold back tears. His friend was dead, and it was because he'd accepted the ring Griffin had offered.

If I'd been smarter, I would have refused.

He buried his face in his hands. His chest ached, and his gut felt like it had been punched. His breath quickened and his eyes welled up. It would be so easy to go into his friend's shack and collapse in despair. He needed to think.

Who cared if monsters killed this person? Who cared if the world ended? John didn't have anyone left in this world who he cared about or who cared about him. He didn't even know who his parents were; his mother had left him on the doorstep of an orphanage.

He'd been mistreated his entire life for being Black. At school and in the group home, he was always punished more harshly than others who did the same thing. For as long as he could remember, he'd felt aching loneliness deep within. He had no connection. No family. No love. Even his date of birth was an educated guess.

The abuse he'd copped from other kids, and many adults, had left their mark. Then there were the suspicious looks from employees who followed him around stores. Those were "decent" people because they didn't insult him to his face or physically threaten him.

No one alive cared about him, and most people either disregarded or actively mistreated him. What reason would he have to care about saving the world or anyone in it?

Griffin.

That was a reason, surely? The only person John cared about had died, and he'd done nothing to stop it. He hadn't even understood what was happening. How stupid was he? How was he supposed to save anything or anyone if he couldn't even save his only friend?

No. Griffin needed this person saved. He needed the ethereals thwarted. He needed the world saved. John might not care about that right now, but his friend had. He needed to respect his friend's wishes. And to do that, he would need to bottle up his emotions, to stow them all away, like he always had. Once he'd saved this person, he could allow himself his grief.

Griffin said John would know where this person was.

He closed his eyes. At first, he only heard the birds and wind through the trees. Then he felt it. A sense. A pull. An anticipation. Like the tense silence before a thunderstorm. He turned to the direction he felt drawn to. It was the same direction Griffin had pointed to earlier. The south-east. He tugged on his leather jacket, patted his pockets, and rubbed the ring on his finger to make sure it was still there. He wasn't used to wearing jewellery.

He set off through the park, away from Griffin Tree Row and back towards the road.

John walked towards the sensation of anticipation for twenty minutes. Night had properly fallen by now. He followed the footpath adjacent to the cemetery and pretended it wasn't at all a creepy place to be at night.

Three taxi drivers pointedly ignored him before he waved one down willing to give him a lift.

After a tense, ten-minute drive, during which John, to the driver's annoyance, had to change the destination more than once, the sense of his target grew stronger. Handing cash to the driver, John stepped into the quiet of a university campus after dark. Sandstone buildings loomed, silent and imposing in the dim evening light. He wandered through the campus, guided by the connection he felt. Within a minute, it led him to a multi-storey edifice: a library. His quarry was somewhere on an upper floor.

The glass doors slid open with a soft hiss, and John stepped into the hushed quiet of the library's foyer. He couldn't remember the last time he'd been in a library, and he'd never been to a university. The loans and reference desks were crewed by a skeleton staff, their faces lit by the soft glow of boxy computer screens.

John moved with purpose, his black leather jacket and cargo pants standing out against the sea of casual student attire. He could feel the curious glances of the students and staff still lingering at this late hour, their eyes drawn to his unfamiliar presence. Ignoring their stares, he followed the pull towards his target, his shoes thudding softly against the carpet as he made his way to the staircase and scaled the stairs two at a time.

The upper floor was even quieter, the rows of bookcases stretching out like a labyrinth, blocking most of the view. The presence felt stronger here, a beacon in the quiet. A sense of anticipation bubbled up inside him, not quite fear, but nervous apprehension. He turned left past the bathrooms, finding himself in a reading area where a handful of students were hunched over their books, scribbling notes in the dim light.

He allowed himself to be drawn along between the reading area and the bookcases, passing by a few solitary students engrossed in their books. He stopped. Apart from these scattered individuals, there was only one person left before him. Seated in the far corner, away from everyone else, was a girl. Twenty or so years old with long, dark hair and Asian features. She was well-dressed by John's standards, with a white button-up shirt and black skirt. A black handbag sat on the desk next to a pile of textbooks, and a black coat was draped over the empty chair beside her.

Maybe she was an international student? That thought gave John pause. If she was born overseas, then how could she have drawn Griffin to this land ages ago? It didn't add up. But before he worried about that discrepancy, he needed to confirm that she was indeed the person he was looking for.

She was engrossed in *Genetics and Molecular Biology of Anaerobic Bacteria*. She chewed the pen in her left hand and frowned at the book like it had personally offended her.

John walked to her with his palms up in what he hoped was a harmless gesture.

"Hi," he said quietly. "My name is—"

She looked up with widened eyes and gasped. "John?" she said.

His eyebrows shot up and his voice caught in his throat. "Uh, yes."

"You scared the shit out of me!" she whispered.

He realised she didn't have a foreign accent; she was from around here. He'd lost count of the times he'd been asked where he was *really* from, as if he hadn't been born in this country. For him to think the same about her made him feel like a presumptuous idiot.

"How do you know who I am?" he asked, unnerved.

She narrowed her eyes at him.

"We went to the same school. You were in a different class, got in trouble heaps, and got kept down a few years."

He flinched as if struck. It was true. Now that he thought about it, she did look familiar.

Jessica … the girl from the wealthy family, always well-dressed and composed.

"Jessica … Brown?"

"Yes," she hissed. "What do you want? I'm trying to study here."

It wasn't supposed to go like this.

Not that he knew how it should have gone. How do you approach a stranger and convince them to go with you because monsters are out to get them? He considered his words.

"You're in danger."

She didn't look convinced. "Uh-huh."

He thought quickly. "There's a gang after you, and if you don't come with me now, they're going to abduct you or worse."

She tilted her head. "A gang? Is this your gang?"

"I'm not in a gang!" he protested.

"You seem like you'd be in a gang, and you're telling me I'm in danger. How could you possibly know that if you aren't part of the gang?"

He was stumped at the question and stung by the accusation. Of course, a spoiled princess like her would assume he was in a gang. His face warmed, and he clenched his fists.

"Look, I'm not in a gang," he said, raising his voice. "I'll explain later how I found this out, but you have to come with me right now. Pretty girls get kidnapped every day. Do you think you're too special for that to happen?"

She looked terrified. But of him, not of unseen gangs. "Get away from me!"

Her voice echoed through the quiet library. People looked over at them.

Oh no, that wasn't the right thing to say.

He was losing her quickly and would fail Griffin. He gritted his teeth.

"Look, I don't know how—"

He felt a yawning, hollow darkness and turned away from Jessica. Ignoring the stares of the other students, he walked along the nearest bookcase, almost in a trance. It was as if something dangerous was pulling him in, his instincts urging him to uncover the source of the threat.

A dishevelled man in his forties emerged from the central stairway John had ascended just minutes ago. His clothes were tattered and torn, and he walked with an oddly stiff, deliberate gait. John felt an emptiness when he stared at the man, like a void. They were in great danger.

The man stared back at John and bared his teeth in a predatory smile.

CHAPTER FIVE

John snapped out of his trance-like state and moved behind the bookshelf.

Griffin was right.

They existed. Ethereal creatures. He *felt* the darkness from the strange man across the library floor. This is what Griffin meant by "dark creature." Not dark in appearance but in essence. His ring finger twitched in response to his presence.

He rushed back to Jessica.

"I get it," he whispered loudly. "You don't trust me. But there's a crazy-looking guy after you *right now*, and if you don't get out of here, I can't protect you."

She bit her lip and regarded him with a serious expression.

"Where is he?" she whispered.

John pointed to the stairwell behind him.

He could feel the dark presence of the dishevelled man moving slowly and deliberately through the middle of the room between the rows of bookshelves. No, not a man, he only looked like one—this was an *ethereal*. John's finger twitched again.

"He's coming."

From the background, the murmur of students rose. Though

their words were indistinct, a shared unease threaded through their whispers, a reaction to the new arrival that echoed John's own feelings.

"How do we get out of here?" Jessica whispered.

John could hear the intention behind her words: as afraid as she was of John, she could also sense the other students' discomfort.

She had a point, though. The stairway was directly behind the ethereal, and they'd have to pass him if they went along the reading area. John looked around desperately.

"Fire exit," John whispered and pointed. "Go, go, go!"

Jessica bolted towards the fire exit, and John hurried after her.

Halfway across the room, the ethereal burst into view. Jessica gasped and froze in place. The ethereal stalked forwards and loomed over her. Jessica froze in place, eyes wide and body rigid. He reached for her with bony hands.

Without thinking, John leaped forwards and took a swing. He missed, and the ethereal stepped back, covering his eyes as if blinded by something bright.

He wouldn't give the ethereal a second chance to grab her. John pushed Jessica towards the fire exit, and they barrelled through the door into a concrete stairwell.

"Go. Go!" John said.

Their shoes shuffled and slapped against the concrete, echoing through the emergency staircase. The fire door slammed shut above them with a deep boom. John could feel Jessica's terror.

They raced to the bottom. The fire door above them smashed open, and the irregular footfalls of the ethereal pummelled the stairs above them. They pushed through the last emergency door and exited into the cool night air.

Jessica took the lead and ran off. John had no idea of the campus layout, so he followed her. Fear fuelled their flight along footpaths, grassy spaces, and asphalt roads as they worked through the maze of buildings. At this time of night, there weren't many students around, so they couldn't hide in a crowd. They passed through areas well-lit by streetlights and darker patches where the night ruled.

John panted and asked, "How can we get out of here? When's the next bus due?"

"Not—not for another twenty minutes," she stammered. Beneath her words, John could feel a flicker of uncertainty, like a hope that she had remembered the bus schedule correctly amidst the chaos.

"We won't last twenty minutes. Do you have a plan?" he asked.

"Ferry," she said.

They ran through the campus, past buildings and trees, across a pedestrian crossing and down a concrete staircase cut into the sloped bank of the nearby river.

The ferry was moored at the pontoon terminal.

She can obviously think on her feet, despite her fear.

They ran across the gangplank. John didn't look back but still felt the dark presence of the ethereal in the distance. He hoped they could board and take off before their pursuer caught up to them.

As they stumbled onto the ferry, Jessica's hand darted to her side, patting the fabric of her skirt in a frantic rhythm. Her eyes widened, a fresh wave of panic washing over her features.

"I ... I ..." she stammered, her voice barely a whisper.

John didn't need her to finish. He understood the gesture, the sudden fear. Her purse. She'd left it in the library. He quickly pulled out his wallet, his heart pounding as he fumbled with the notes. He paid for their tickets, his wallet noticeably lighter than it had been at the start of the night. He could feel the ethereal's presence growing closer, adding a franticness to his movements.

"Just keep moving," he hissed.

After the taxi fare and ferry tickets, he was painfully aware he didn't have much money left. Not enough for a taxi ride back to the shack. One crisis at a time.

They moved to the rear of the ferry and looked at the university campus.

"He's coming," John said.

"Are you sure?" she asked, eyes wild.

"I'm sure."

"Why is he after me?" she asked. Her eyes watered. Or were they tears?

"It's a long story. I just hope we leave before he gets here. How long does this thing wait for, anyway?"

"Shouldn't be long now," she said. She didn't sound convinced.

"I really hope you're right," he said.

Jessica chewed her nails. John's ring finger twitched.

"Can you swim?" he asked.

"Yes," she said, then opened her eyes wide in alarm. "Why?"

John ground his teeth together. "He's almost here. If the boat doesn't move soon, we might have to swim for it."

Jessica swore under her breath, "Chết tiệt."

John didn't understand the language, but he understood her meaning: shit.

Jessica covered her mouth and paced back and forth, freaking out. He was surprised she'd kept it together so well so far.

John looked about and considered options. There weren't any more passengers left to board, but the ferry still hadn't moved. He might have to do something drastic. He had no idea how to drive a boat, but to save Jessica, he might have to figure it out. With a sigh, he walked towards the cabin.

The boat's engines spun up and the ferry jerked forward. John caught himself on the doorway at the sudden lurch. They were pulling away from the terminal. They were going to make it. Maybe?

"Look!" Jessica called out.

John's finger twitched. The ethereal had caught up, but the ferry had already moved far enough from the terminal that he couldn't board it.

The ethereal stared at them, his expression blank. He no longer smiled.

"That's really fucking creepy," Jessica said under her breath. She looked at John with a pained expression.

"You're not wrong."

John looked back at the bank, but the ethereal was gone. He searched for signs of him on the shore or in the water.

"This feels even worse."

"Who was that?" she asked.

"Nashgrakh," he replied flatly and automatically.

"Nash ... grakh?" she asked.

"I, uh, I think it's his name," John said.

"Who told you that?" she asked.

He didn't have an answer for her. It didn't even sound like a name, so why did he think it was?

"Who's Yondarel?" she asked.

"Yondarel?"

"You just said that's who told you his name."

He frowned. "I ... didn't say that. I didn't say anything."

She stared at him.

"Yes, you did."

He must have said the name out loud; he sensed the truth in her words. How did he know Nashgrakh's name? Who was Yondarel? He felt exposed and vulnerable.

"Did I?"

"I don't remember you being like this."

"Like what?" he asked.

"This weird."

He sighed. "It's been a hell of a day." He reached into his pocket and pulled out his cigarette kit.

"What are you doing?" she asked with a hint of panic.

"Rolling a cigarette. What does it look like?"

"No smoking on the ferry. See?" She pointed to the sign with a shaky finger. The sign, illuminated by the ferry's soft interior lights, clearly depicted a cigarette with a red line through it.

"Fuck."

He angrily stuffed it back in his pocket. Smoking usually helped him think and focus. Now, he was left with the cool evening air flowing over him as the ferry picked up speed, the low hum of the engine and the occasional murmur of other passengers the only sounds breaking the silence.

"Okay," he said after a minute's thought, his gaze drifting over the sparse crowd of late-night commuters and the city's distant lights reflecting on the water. "I'm assuming this takes us to the city?"

She looked around nervously. "It's about twenty minutes. Four stops along the way."

"Right, well, let's hope they don't think ahead and catch us at one of the stops."

"They?" she asked.

"I'm sure there are more. It's not just that guy."

"Nashgrakh," she said flatly.

"Yes, him. There'll be others, too. When we get to the city, we should head into the centre to lose them and maybe catch a bus back across the river to the suburbs."

"Why are you doing this?" Jessica asked.

He looked at her in surprise. "What?"

"Why are you trying to keep me safe?"

John rubbed his temples in exasperation. "What do you mean?"

"The John I knew never did anything for anyone. What do you want from me?"

"Nothing," he said. He hoped she'd drop it. He wasn't in the mood for this conversation.

"Nothing?"

"Yes, that's what I said. I just need to keep you safe."

"If you think I'm going to do anything for you out of gratitude—"

"You don't have anything to worry about." He understood; he could feel the worry behind her words. "Not interested, thanks."

She looked relieved. The silence grew between them. And the awkwardness.

The cool air from the river rushed past them.

"It's cold," Jessica said, rubbing her arms.

John looked at her short sleeves and exposed arms and shook his head. "Maybe you should have worn a jacket."

"I did, but it's back in the library, along with my bag and money and ID and everything else."

John grimaced and rubbed the back of his neck. "Yeah, I forgot about that."

He only had the leftover money from Griffin. If he'd had his own money, his life would have been so much easier. Jessica had money. Of course she did. If only they'd thought to bring it.

John realised he didn't feel cold. He sighed and took off his leather jacket, handing it to her wordlessly.

Jessica tentatively took it from him. She lacked John's broad shoulders, so it was far too big on her, but she looked comfortable.

"Thank you."

John grunted in reply. He could feel she was being genuine, and it made him uncomfortable.

He contemplated the cold breeze. It was odd that he didn't feel cold. Griffin never wore warm clothes, and his shack didn't have a fireplace or heater. Maybe an effect of wearing the ring. John looked at his hand and the innocuous-looking piece of jewellery.

"Are you going to tell me why you're helping me?" Jessica asked.

John could feel the intention beyond her words. She didn't seem suspicious or apprehensive this time.

"I just want to understand why you're helping me, is all," she repeated.

John shifted uncomfortably. He wondered how much he could safely tell her. He didn't want to scare her off again.

"Look, a friend wanted me to help you out, that's all. I don't really want to talk about it right now."

"Who is it?"

He couldn't bring himself to talk about Griffin yet. He shook his head.

"I've got a question for you. Why do you wear such impractical clothing?"

"Excuse me?" she said.

"Your skirt."

"My skirt?"

"And those ballerina slipper things you're wearing."

"They're called flats."

"Right. Not exactly the best clothing when you need to run for your life."

"Well, I'm sorry I wasn't expecting to have to run for my life today," she said.

"That must be nice," he shot back.

They fell into awkward silence. John was fine with that. It hurt too much to talk about Griffin.

The ferry continued along the river for several minutes before slowly approaching the next terminal. John tensed. He scoured the terminal but couldn't sense any threats. Next to him, Jessica stared at the shore and chewed her lip. He once again felt her fear.

Minutes passed, passengers disembarked and embarked, and the ferry continued on its way. The next three stops were similarly uneventful.

They reached the city terminal.

CHAPTER SIX

John and Jessica rushed off the ferry, across the gangway, and up the stairs towards the city.

They seemed to be safe. John couldn't sense any darkness about them, so they headed further up the bank. A tense but uneventful eight-minute walk through the city centre brought them to a bus stop. He'd deliberately steered them away from the open-air pedestrian mall as he wasn't confident in his ability to sense danger if people were around.

John approached the bus stop sign and ran his index finger down the list of stops. "This is where we need to go," he said, pointing to their destination on the sign. "We'll then have to walk several blocks, but I think this will get us ahead of any pursuers and buy us the time we'll need."

Jessica scrutinised the sign. "But the next bus won't be for half an hour."

"Yeah, that is a problem." John looked around anxiously. "Maybe we should keep moving and find somewhere to lay low until the bus arrives."

Jessica agreed, and they headed back to the city centre and warily approached an indoor shopping centre adjacent to the pedestrian mall. All the shops were closed except for the super-market, so the sliding doors opened to admit them to the dark and mostly empty building.

John was painfully aware of the CCTV cameras but decided to risk it and led Jessica to a café that opened directly into a food court. The counters were covered, and the chairs had been placed on the tables. The pair sat on the floor in the far corner, out of sight of the main thoroughfare. John crossed his legs and leaned his head on his hand. Jessica sat off to the side with her legs together.

"John," she said.

He could feel her trying to hide her fear.

"Yes?"

"Why are people after me?"

He considered the question. "It's a long story."

"We have time right now."

He sighed. "True."

He tried to work out how much to tell her and where to even start.

"Do you know Griffin Pembroke?" he asked.

"The homeless old hermit?"

"He wasn't homeless!" John replied loudly. Too loudly. He winced at his loudness. Of course, someone with as privileged an upbringing as hers—nice house, caring family—would think of Griffin that way. "He had a home. That shack was his home for longer than we've been alive."

"I'm sorry. Please continue."

"Griffin was the one who told me you were in danger. He gave me all the information, or at least some of it, and wanted me to take you somewhere safe."

"Why did he tell you this? What's his interest?"

John felt at a loss to answer. How could he explain that Griffin was a centuries-old hunter who'd travelled across the sea to find and protect her?

Jessica interrupted his thoughts. "Why don't we go to the police?"

"What?" John said flatly.

"There's a police station a few blocks away from here. If we go to them, they can keep me safe."

John considered how to approach this tactfully. "That would probably just get the police killed and you as well."

She looked at him with suspicion. "How very convenient."

He sighed. "Okay, okay. I can see I'm going to have to tell you more, but you won't believe it anyway."

"Uh-huh," she said flatly.

He didn't want her to run off into danger, so he had to handle this carefully.

John looked around the darkened café, thinking of a way to prove his story. His eyes lit up.

"Hey, do you speak any foreign languages?"

She narrowed her eyes at him. "Why, because I'm Asian?"

"Oh," he said, crestfallen. He'd put his foot in his mouth again.

She sighed. "Yes, I do. Why do you ask?"

He didn't know whether to feel validated or embarrassed.

"Okay, say something in … just say something I shouldn't be able to understand."

She stared at him for a long moment before saying, *"Tôi sẽ rất ngạc nhiên nếu bạn có thể hiểu ngôn ngữ của mẹ tôi."*

He paused and closed his eyes. The words clattered incomprehensibly upon his ears, but he listened beyond to the meaning behind the sounds.

"You said something like you doubt I can understand this," he said.

She looked surprised. "Okay, so you learned a second language. Most people in the world do that, except in this country."

"Oh," he said, eyes downcast. He didn't speak any other

languages and had hoped the demonstration would prove his point. His eyes widened as a thought came to him.

"Here, hold this." John slid the ring off and placed it in her hand. "Actually, better yet, put it on and watch me."

She looked for a moment like she would object but instead sighed, checked its size, and slid it onto her middle finger.

The pain returned with his wounds. His lip and eyebrow split, and bruises returned to his face and body.

She gasped at him.

"Not a pretty sight, hey?" John said. He suspected this might have been a suitably dramatic demonstration. His shoulders slumped forward, burdened by an invisible load that seemed to press him further into his battered body.

"I don't understand," she said.

"Give me the ring."

She did so, and he slid it back on, sighing in relief as his skin zipped back up and the pain and discomfort left.

"Ta-da," he said.

Jessica looked at John's face, then down at her lap. She was silent for a few moments.

"That's ... that's not possible." Her voice was barely audible, her calmness hanging by a thread.

John gave her a moment to recover.

"That man who was after you isn't actually a person," John said. "He's more of a body-snatching monster."

She furrowed her brow, her mouth opening and closing as if struggling to find words.

"I know, I know," he said, hands up in defence. "I didn't believe it either, but seeing is believing. Or I guess *feeling* is believing."

"I don't understand ..." Jessica's voice trailed off, her fingers nervously twisting a strand of her hair.

"Griffin called them 'ethereal beings' and said they were a ... what was it? An 'infestance.'"

Jessica's eyes flicked to his, a frown creasing her forehead. "I don't think that's a word, John."

"Yeah, yeah, I know, but it's how he described them. A malignance, a pestilence, a plague ..."

Jessica held her head like it ached.

"But it's real, or some of it must be," John said. "For instance, what you said before in another language? I don't know how to speak it, but wearing this let me understand your meaning. Also, I didn't know you were studying to become a doctor."

She looked dubious. "Microbiology. Different department."

"Right, all of that. I didn't know that." He paused. "I guessed because of your textbook. But my point is that I put the ring on and could sense your general direction. I know how that sounds, believe me, but it's true. I also felt the presence of that ethereal before I knew he was there."

"So, you're saying it's a magic ring?" she asked.

"Shit, I don't know. I guess? It's just Griffin told me to put on the damned ring, find you, and get you to safety." John's face felt hot; he sounded ridiculous. "He didn't tell me everything. I know that for sure. We were short on time, and I only just got to you. If he'd explained everything, you'd probably be dead by now."

Silence fell between them. John was sick of defending something he knew sounded crazy, and Jessica looked like she was processing.

"Thank you," she said earnestly. "For saving me."

John nodded awkwardly; he wasn't used to thanks or appreciation. "Uh, you're welcome, I guess."

"So, will Griffin explain this more when we get to him?" she asked.

It was like a punch in the gut.

"No," John croaked. He cleared his throat. "He's dead. He died when he took the ring off. Been alive too long, I guess."

More silence.

"I'm sorry, John," Jessica said gently, "I didn't know. He was obviously very special to you."

John nodded silently and blinked back tears.

Boys don't cry.

The thought came unbidden, a mantra of his childhood. In a neighbourhood where his dark skin made him a minority, he already stood out enough. Showing weakness always brought trouble. For a young boy, crying was a luxury he'd never been able to afford.

The mantra helped him now, though. It was familiar. He had to keep it together until he got Jessica to safety. He could fall to pieces afterwards.

Something was wrong.

"Wait," John said.

The sensation was similar to the yawning darkness he'd felt in the library but more confused. It felt like being blinded by a spotlight.

Jessica looked at him, alarmed.

Glass smashed as two people burst through the shopping centre doors and fell to the ground, clawing at each other. They looked like a man in his twenties and an elderly woman, but John knew that was a lie. They were ethereals. The young man's essence was dark, like the one from the library. John instinctively knew his name was Yekhtreshk. The old woman, her presence blinding in comparison, was Zeluniel. How he knew this didn't matter. All that mattered was Jessica.

The two ethereals grappled with each other. In the midst of their struggle, there was a brief pause as they each tried to get the upper hand. In that moment, John noticed a glint of gold on the old woman's hand. Zeluniel bore a gold ring on the middle finger of her right hand. As the fight resumed, she raised it in a fist and punched Yekhtreshk, but he dodged and bit down on her wrist, wrapping his hands around her throat. She bashed at his face with her other hand. He pushed her to the ground, his teeth latching onto her arm like a mad dog.

"Jessica, run!" John yelled.

He pointed at the broken doors. On the street, they stood a chance but trapped in the shopping centre, they didn't.

Jessica bolted for the entrance, past the fighters. Yekhtreshk saw her and abandoned the old woman, leaping towards Jessica. John sprinted forward, closing the gap between them in a few strides. With a burst of adrenaline, he swung his right fist and smashed Yekhtreshk in the face. The man screamed, shrill and inhuman, and fell to the ground, clutching his face. It wasn't bruised or bloody. It was *burned*.

"Yondarel?" the old woman said to John. "You got away from the killer?"

"Get back!" John screamed at her.

Zeluniel clambered to her feet and eyed him cautiously. She kept her eyes on John and stepped over to the screaming man, stomping on his throat and holding her foot down. The screams were replaced with sickening gurgles. She looked at John's hand with an enigmatic expression.

John raced through the entrance onto the street.

The broken doors impotently closed after him; they wouldn't stop Zeluniel.

He looked back. She was still holding Yekhtreshk down. John took advantage and sprinted down the street in pursuit of Jessica, who had a block's head start on him. Behind him, an inhuman scream echoed into the night, loud as a thunderclap. It ceased just as quickly. John could no longer feel the sensation of darkness, only brightness. He ran on.

CHAPTER SEVEN

John followed Jessica to a bus stop at the end of the block. A bus waited, but its doors were closed. He caught up and watched Jessica loudly plead with the driver through the closed glass door. John tried to make himself unnoticeable. Jessica had a chance to persuade the driver, but if the driver saw him, they'd drive off like the taxis.

She must have convinced the driver because the doors opened. Jessica stepped onboard and thanked the driver profusely. John moved quickly and stepped in behind her. The driver narrowed his eyes at him, his gaze lingering. He opened his mouth to object, so John handed over the money for their tickets. The driver hesitated, looking at the money as if it were counterfeit, before grudgingly accepting it. Ignoring the driver's foul expression and the unspoken prejudice hanging in the air, John grabbed his ticket and headed towards the back of the bus, wanting to put as much space as possible between himself and the driver. Jessica followed.

There were a handful of other passengers on the bus, but he didn't sense any threat from them. A sign on the rear window said, "In case of emergency, break glass."

John stared out the window. He could still feel Zeluniel's presence like a searchlight. She drew nearer, but he couldn't see her yet. The bus took off, and he breathed a sigh of relief. As long as it didn't stop at too many red lights, Zeluniel couldn't reach them on foot.

They weren't travelling the route they wanted, but whatever got them away from here would do for now. He only had loose change left. They would have to ride the bus out of the city until he felt safe enough to get off and find another way to Griffin's shack. How long would it take on foot? Probably too long.

Police sirens blared in the distance. John looked around out of habit, but they were probably responding to the disturbance in the shopping centre.

His mind wandered back to Griffin and his shack. The city council had, for many years, wanted to level Griffin's shack and remove the longstanding eyesore from their leafy neighbour-hood. But it had stood there, and Griffin had dwelt within it, for seemingly time immemorial. Griffin's Tree Row was probably a large part of keeping the peace: the neighbourhood residents and the council were happy that it obscured the shack from the view of street goers, and Griffin had been happy for the privacy.

Griffin had explained to John that he'd signed an agreement with the city council, smoothing the legal pathway to reclaim the land upon his death. John remembered how he'd chuckled when he told him the story. It had been a terrible deal for the council. It was now decades later, and the mayor and councillors had all retired. Every new mayor and councillor assumed he would die of natural causes during their term if they waited just a little longer. And as the decades passed, the politicians came and went, yet Griffin Pembroke had remained, apparently unmoved by time itself.

John's eyes misted up. Time had caught up with Griffin after all. He wondered how long the city council would take to realise Griffin was gone and to reclaim the land.

What had that old woman, that ethereal, called John? Yondarel? He shuddered. And what did she mean when she asked if he'd "got away from the killer?" He had the distinct impression she meant Griffin. Had Griffin killed ethereals? Is that what she meant? He felt that wasn't right and that his subconscious knew the answers. He was too exhausted to work it out right now.

The sirens faded into the distance as the bus drove on.

"When we get off, I want to find a payphone," Jessica said.

"Why?" John asked. He dragged his attention away from his thoughts.

"I need to tell my family I'm okay."

Life would have been so much easier if I'd had a family.

"Well, you're not okay yet," he said, scowling. "Besides, what will you tell them? 'Hi, remember that delinquent, John Wedgewood? We're being chased by monsters. Don't wait up!'"

"They'll be worried if I don't check in."

"I have no idea what that's like," John said.

A silence grew between them.

"So ..." Jessica said.

"Yes?"

"Wedgewood?"

He tensed, knowing what question was coming. The rumour had followed him throughout his school years, and he'd never confirmed nor denied it.

"Yes, I'm named after the old orphanage," he said.

"Oh," she said.

"Some sick bastard wanted to call me John Doe, but thankfully someone else decided not to name me after an unidentified person," he said, then stared, unfocused, at the seat in front of him.

His time at the Wedgewood Institute was short-lived as the state closed the orphanages and moved the children into group homes. John was lonely and isolated despite being one of many children in the home. No one had wanted to foster or adopt a "problem child," so he remained as younger children came and went. Eventually, he turned eighteen, and the state didn't have to care about him anymore.

John made a bitter expression. "Instead, I was branded with a name that told everyone I was unwanted and unloved."

"That's not true," Jessica said.

"Really? I think I know my own life," he said.

"I meant that no one ever loved you."

"I can't have mattered to anyone else, or someone would have adopted me. Or one of my parents would have kept me."

"They must have had their reasons."

"Fuck their reasons. I don't know who they are and don't want to know. I don't even care if they're alive."

The look on her face told him he'd overreacted. Again. Some of the passengers turned around and stared. He felt bad but lowered his head and crossed his arms.

"I'm sorry," Jessica said quietly. "I didn't realise it was such a painful topic, and I should have."

"It's not a painful topic. It just makes me angry," he lied, forcing his eyes to stop watering. He had to keep it together and get her to safety. Once she was safe, he could grieve. Then he could fall apart.

Something landed on the roof of the bus with a bang.

The passengers reacted with shock, but John could sense the danger. A darkness washed over him. His ring finger felt restless.

"It's Nashgrakh," John said. "He's back."

"But how?" she whispered. "How the hell did he get on the roof?"

The bus continued through the city; the driver seemingly determined not to stop moving in the bustling evening traffic.

John looked around frantically. What was Nashgrakh planning? Would he try something on a moving bus in front of all these people?

His eyes came to rest on the "In case of emergency, break glass" sign. This might be such an emergency.

The back window exploded inward, and glass fragments flew into the bus as Nashgrakh leaped in. He grinned with satisfaction as he moved towards Jessica, but John stepped between them.

The bus lurched, and passengers screamed. John and Nashgrakh gripped the headrests on either side of the aisle and remained steady on their feet.

Jessica bolted towards the front but tripped over a backpack, falling to the floor awkwardly. John ignored her and faced the ethereal. He had to buy her some time. He tried staring Nashgrakh down, but when he stalked forward John ran at him. Nashgrakh batted him aside with ease, smashing him through a window onto the road.

The bus's brakes shrieked, and it lurched to a stop.

John hit the asphalt hard, the impact jarring every bone in his body. Despite the ring, pain exploded, sharp and immediate. He rolled several times, the momentum carrying him along the rough surface, ripping open his skin and clothes. Cars swerved and honked, and tyres screeched as drivers dodged him. A car smashed into the back of the bus with a loud crunch and shattered glass.

John struggled to catch his breath, the sting of fresh wounds all over his body. He clutched his side and crawled off the road, blood dripping onto the ground. Within seconds, his cuts and bruises healed. He staggered to his feet and ran. A mass of people flooded out of the bus, while John fought his way inside to reach Jessica. He had to stop the monster.

Jessica cowered on the floor, clutching her ankle. The ethereal stood over her and grasped at her. John jumped at him and swung his fist at his head. Nashgrakh shrieked and fell back, face burned. John grabbed Jessica's hand and yanked her to her feet.

They ran blindly into the street with the rest of the panicked crowd.

They ran through the city streets, panting and exhausted. Sirens echoed through the night behind them. After several minutes, they reached the railway station, a major junction where the city lines met. They were bound to find a train here.

John caught his breath first, thanks to the ring, and Jessica had a stitch. He didn't have enough money for train tickets, but that had never stopped him before.

He looked to Jessica, who crouched and rubbed her sore ankle.

"Come on. The next train isn't for fifty minutes, and we're too exposed out here."

"What"—she grabbed her side and took a breath—"what now?"

"We need to lay low for a bit," John said. He glanced around. "There's bound to be a hotel nearby. Should buy us a few minutes if anyone tracks us down."

She nodded. And, gripping her side with a pained expression, followed him through the night.

Chapter Eight

They reached a suitable-looking hotel, a five-storey, brown brick building near the station. John had no money for a room, but he had a plan.

They walked into a brightly lit reception area full of chairs and a stand of pamphlets. A young woman with a cascade of playful red curls appeared and greeted them at the counter. Her eyes sparkled with a zest for life that John couldn't believe someone working this late at night would have. A badge on her shirt read, "Samantha".

"Hi," John said. He forced a smile and waved awkwardly. "Do you have any rooms free?"

Samantha looked at John, then at Jessica. "Is that a room for two?"

"Uh, yes. Please," he said. He shifted uncomfortably.

The receptionist smiled knowingly.

"Do you have a booking?"

"No. I ... no, we don't."

"That's okay," she said. "I have a queen room on the top floor with a great view of the park."

She must have assumed they were a couple. Jessica wore an

oversized jacket that was clearly his. Two young people—a Black guy and an Asian girl, no less—without luggage after a room in the middle of the night. He felt uncomfortable, imagining the assumptions she might make, and wanted to correct her.

"That sounds lovely," Jessica said. "Doesn't it, dear?"

Jessica and Samantha looked at him.

"… absolutely," he said.

"Great!" Samantha said, looking amused. "I need to take an imprint of your credit card for incidentals."

John frantically rifled through his pockets and handed her a credit card. A flicker of worry passed through him. Would she notice it wasn't his? Would they have to make a run for it if she called the police?

The receptionist ran the card through an imprinter, making a heavy *chunk chunk*. She collected the carbon paper copy and handed over the card and a key.

"Have a good evening, Mr Phillips," she said with a wry smile. "Please enjoy your stay."

John exhaled loudly with relief.

"Uh, thanks, you too."

"Thank you, Samantha, you've been wonderful," Jessica said as she steered John into the elevator.

"What did—"

"Đợi một lát," Jessica said quietly but insistently.

He understood: wait a minute.

The elevator dinged, and they stepped into the hallway. Jessica grabbed the key from him and walked ahead, unlocking the room.

John opened his mouth to talk, but Jessica spoke first.

"A young couple looking for privacy attracts a lot less attention than two strangers on the run from monsters."

He closed his mouth.

That's a good point.

Jessica sat on the queen-size bed and removed her shoes. She massaged her ankle and winced. John sat on a chair at a desk next to the boxy TV.

"So," she said coyly, "Mr Phillips …?"

"Yeah, yeah," he said. "I do odd jobs for people sometimes, and one guy gave me this card as payment. It probably doesn't work, but it looks legit and hasn't expired yet."

"Uh-huh."

"By the time they realise it doesn't work, we'll be long gone. We only need to wait another thirty minutes, then head back to the train. I think a bit of fraud is acceptable when I have no money and am trying to save your life."

And the world …

"I appreciate that, and thank you," she said. "I'm just not used to any of this. I'm not used to taking part in illegal activities."

John bristled at her wording.

"I'm sorry," she said, hands raised in front of her. "I think it's really cool you did that for me."

John sighed, and his anger left him.

He leaned to the side and pulled out his cigarette kit. Jessica wrinkled her nose at the sight of it.

"Jesus Christ," he said defensively.

She shrugged. "It's just horrible and will probably kill you."

"Life's not that great anyway. Why prolong it?"

She looked horrified and then pointed to the "No Smoking" sign over the door and the smoke detector on the ceiling.

"Oh, for fuck's sake!" He shoved the kit back in his pocket and sat in sullen silence for a minute. "By the way, your makeup's running."

"Oh, shit."

She jumped up and went into the bathroom. John stewed in silence, tapping his leg irritably. Five minutes later, she returned with no makeup and slumped onto the bed.

"Who were you trying to impress at the library, of all places?" he asked.

"Excuse me?"

"You were studying by yourself. Why were you wearing makeup?"

"What the hell are you talking about?"

"Which guy were you trying to impress?"

She had a "what the fuck?" look on her face. "I don't wear it to look good for anyone. I do it for myself."

"Yeah, right." He rolled his eyes.

"It makes me feel more confident," she explained, her voice rising slightly, and her hands balled into fists at her sides.

"Because it makes you more appealing to men?" he shot back. "Or you're trying to fit in with other girls? One of those, anyway."

Her eyes flashed with rage. "Okay, why do you have short hair, then?"

"What?"

"If you're so above caring about other people's perception of you, why not grow your hair long?"

"It's not the same."

"Explain to me how it's not the same."

Because he would have stood out more if he hadn't kept it short. People thought he was being deliberately difficult by making his hair stand up instead of sitting flat. He kept it short to avoid the attention.

In other words, to fit in.

He looked at the floor sullenly. "I guess ... I guess I keep it short to avoid trouble. To fit in."

She looked at him carefully. "How we present ourselves to the world is something we get to choose. No one else should get a say."

"I get it now," he said, his voice carefully neutral. He didn't really believe her, but he was sick of the discussion and so raised his hands in defeat. "I'd never really thought about it that way before." He hoped she'd drop the subject and stop talking now.

She sighed and looked exasperated. "You're not the only one. My family keeps trying to set me up with guys, but between work and studying, I barely have time to myself. They don't understand. My mother, mostly. She's pushed me so hard for so long to be the best at school, get into the best university, get a good degree, get a good job. Second place was always a failure. I had to be number one. Anything but perfect marks meant I wasn't trying hard enough. She just wants me to be the best I can be and have a better life than she did. And I've done it, but it takes so much time and energy. And on top of that, she expects me to date!"

She doesn't have the same risk of being bashed to death on a semi-regular basis. "Yeah, life's tough being a goody-two-shoes. 'I'm too busy to get a date.' Please."

Her mouth dropped open. "It's not just about time. Maybe dating should mean something special, too?"

He laughed. "Sex doesn't have any deeper meaning. It's just for fun."

"Really?" she said. "How many girls have you 'had fun' with, then?"

"Zero."

She had an uncharacteristically smug expression on her face. "Ha! Then you're as much of a goody-two-shoes as I am."

"I'm not."

"Sounds like you are."

He looked her in the eye, a defiant spark in his gaze. He wasn't about to let her turn the tables on him. "I'm not a virgin."

He maintained eye contact with her while she processed that, a hint of satisfaction creeping into his expression at her surprise as she understood what he meant.

"Oh," she said after a moment. "I didn't know."

"That's because I don't want anyone to know. No one gives a damn about me, so they don't get to know anything about me.

And besides," he said while he looked at the floor, "the more people know, the more they have to hurt you with."

She walked over and put her hand on his shoulder. He didn't look up. He wanted to vent, not be pitied.

"Something I've never understood," he said, "is how the number of girls you sleep with is associated with manliness."

She sat and looked confused.

"Given that I don't want to and never will, why does that make me unmanly? I could be the toughest son of a bitch in the world, but that wouldn't count for anything."

She shrugged. "If you're asking me why society and culture set these standards, I've got no idea."

She seemed to sense his discomfort and changed the subject.

"So, these ethereal creatures can take over a person's body?"

"Yeah," John said, "it's apparently the only way they can affect the world. I don't know the details, though."

"How would I tell if one took over your body?"

John thought for a few moments. "I'm pretty sure they have to take over a dead body. But yeah, if they kill me, I guess they could take over my body and come after you with it. Pretty fucking horrifying. I mean, in addition to being brutally murdered, that is."

"We should use a passphrase so I know you're definitely you."

John nodded. "Like what?"

"What about trivia? Something every person who's not secretly a monster will know."

"Good idea."

"How about … Which city hosted the Olympics last year?"

He gave her a blank look.

"What?" she asked.

"How the hell would I know that?" he asked.

"Oh," she said, deflated. "I thought everyone knew."

"I don't watch TV," he said. "I don't read newspapers. I don't even have a radio."

"I'm sorry, I thought it was a universal thing."

"So?" he asked.

"So, what?"

"Which city hosted the Olympics last year?"

"Oh! Barcelona."

"In Spain?"

"Yeah."

"Right. Barcelona."

Silence fell upon the room. John didn't mind it but felt uncomfortable just sitting around. He looked at the alarm clock on the bedside table. They still had fifteen minutes to kill before they could safely leave.

"So …" Jessica eventually said. "Do you have a boyfriend?"

"No," he said. Eager to deflect the conversation away from his personal life, he quickly turned the question back on her. "You?"

"No. And I got bullied a lot at school for it."

"I doubt it."

She looked shocked.

He laughed. "I doubt anyone's called *you* a 'fag' or bashed your face in."

"No, only 'bitch', 'slut', 'frigid' and emotionally torture me. Much better!"

"Oh, please. So, some kids were mean to you. You've had a cushy life handed to you on a silver platter."

She stood, enraged. "I've had to work hard for everything I've done. My mother nearly died in a boat coming to this country. That's why she's so desperate for me to have a better life than she did. I nearly had a mental breakdown last year!"

He realised he'd crossed a line. Several, in fact. He didn't know what to say; Griffin was the only person he'd felt comfortable apologising to.

"You have no idea what school is like for girls," she continued. "Or how vicious they can be. I was constantly bullied for being gay."

She clearly wouldn't wear makeup to look hot for guys if she wasn't into them.

"I didn't know," he whispered, feeling a pang of guilt for his earlier assumptions.

"No one does, and I'm not even gay, either. I can't imagine how much harder it would have been if I was."

John blinked in surprise. He had jumped to conclusions twice now, and it was a stark reminder of how little he really knew about her. He felt a mix of confusion and embarrassment. He, of all people, should know not to take rumours at face value, even though they were rumours she shared with him herself.

"At least you have a family to support you. No one's ever loved me, not even my mother. What's the expression? 'Someone only a mother could love.' Well, that wasn't me. I wasn't even loved enough by her."

After another minute of silence, Jessica spoke up. "I guess everyone's broken in their own way. Like different patterns in shattered glass."

He pondered that. "Then why put in so much effort? If life is so hard, why make all those fancy plans? University? Work? Why bother?"

She looked confused. "If you don't make plans, you'll never get anything you want. Are you saying you don't make plans?"

"No. What's the point?"

"Well, what do you live for? What gets you out of bed in the morning?"

He thought carefully for a moment. "Spite, mostly."

"I don't understand."

"I exist in life," he said, putting the thoughts together as he went, "purely to spite those who look down on me. I have nothing to aspire to and no great plans. The best I can hope for is that my continued existence makes the people who hate me unhappy. A thorn in their side."

Jessica looked sad. "You say that, and I'm sure you believe it," she said softly, "but I don't think you're quite as misanthropic as you think."

"What is it about anything I've said that gives you that impression?" he asked, bewildered.

"Look where you are right now. You put your life on the line to save me, someone you don't really know. Would a bitter misanthrope save anyone other than himself?"

She was wrong. He was a miserable bastard. He hated life, and everyone still left in it. That's who he was. With Griffin gone, life was a hostile place with no refuge. Who did she think she was?

"I need a smoke," he said, grabbing the room key.

John stepped out of the elevator on the ground floor and past the now-vacant reception into the cool night air. The full moon shone. It was the only thing he could see in the sky due to the city lights.

He tried to roll a cigarette, but his hands shook, so he gave up, frustrated. Maybe the fresh air would calm him instead.

The hair stood up on the back of his neck and arms. Something was wrong. He could feel Jessica's presence all the way through the hotel walls, stronger than before. And if he could sense it, the ethereals would as well.

He raced back to the hotel but froze.

He felt a familiar brightness.

Zeluniel had found them.

CHAPTER NINE

John raced into the hotel elevator.

Zeluniel's presence felt brighter than when he last saw her. Instead of a spotlight, it felt like a lighthouse. He knew she was approaching the building.

The elevator took an excruciatingly long time to reach the top floor. John tapped his foot impatiently. When it finally dinged open, he pushed the buttons for every floor except ground, then raced to their room. He jiggled the handle. Locked. Of course it was. He unlocked it and then rushed inside.

Jessica wasn't on the bed. She wasn't in the room. His skin felt cold.

The toilet flushed.

Oh, thank God.

He bashed on the door. "We've gotta go!" he yelled. "Now!"

"Wait a minute!"

Jessica opened the door a moment later. She looked terrified. "Come on!" John said.

He opened the door carefully and checked the corridor. Clear for now.

They ran to the fire exit and got through it just as the elevator dinged.

The staircase had a chain-link fence along the sides. Breathing heavily, they raced down four flights of stairs into the concrete car park and towards the nearby park. John looked back. Zeluniel watched them from the top of the stairs.

John and Jessica ran across the grassy park towards the railway terminal. Jessica was in the lead, and John followed closely. He felt the familiar dark sensation, and his ring finger cramped.

John slammed into the ground; the air knocked out of him. The world spun for a moment before he rolled onto his back, gasping for breath.

Half of Nashgrakh's face was blackened and burned. No grin this time. He bared his teeth.

John swung his right fist, but Nashgrakh pinned his arm easily and pushed him harder into the ground. John kicked his legs and writhed, crying out as his shoulder dislocated. The creature brought his face closer; he felt like prey in a predator's embrace.

A wave of panic washed over him, not his own, but Yondarel's. It was a sensation, a feeling of dread that echoed his own fear.

"Hey!" Jessica shouted.

Nashgrakh looked up, and she smashed him across the face with a large branch.

The distraction was enough. John brought the ring to Nashgrakh's arm who roared in pain as his flesh sizzled. John wriggled free.

Jessica ran, and Nashgrakh loped after her. John clambered to his feet and followed. After a few steps, his shoulder popped back into place and healed itself. He ran faster.

Nashgrakh dove at Jessica's legs, tripping and knocking her to the ground. He slowly and deliberately dragged her by the ankle to a nearby signpost as she struggled and screamed. He ripped the metal pole from the ground, a mass of concrete around its base. He held it above her.

Jessica screamed as Nashgrakh swung the pole. John jumped between them and held up his forearm to block the blow. With a sickening crunch, his forearm bones splintered and cracked. He roared in pain.

Nashgrakh dropped the pole and grabbed John by the throat, jerking him to his feet. John gasped for breath as Nashgrakh squeezed with both hands.

With a wet pop, the bones in John's arm snapped back into place, unbroken. With an enraged expression, John punched Nashgrakh in the head and fell to the ground awkwardly. He dry-retched as his ankle snapped and almost immediately healed. He tasted reflux, but the air tasted sweet as he breathed freely again.

Nashgrakh clawed at the new burn on his head.

John went to hit him again but froze mid-motion when the ethereal glared at him and snarled. It was a sound that echoed from the depths of a nightmare, a primal warning that set John into flight.

He ran towards the railway tunnel, deliberately leading Nashgrakh away from Jessica, and quickly climbed over the fence and embankment. Nashgrakh leaped clear over and chased him. John ran into the dark tunnel, its darkness swallowing him whole, only several strides ahead of the monster. The rough, uneven walls and the foreboding darkness within felt like he was burrowing beneath the earth.

John ran blindly through the darkness. He hoped Nashgrakh couldn't see in the dark. A distant, low rumble echoed in the distance, and he realised he'd need to time this carefully.

A sudden, brutal force slammed into John's side. Pain

exploded through his body as he was hurled sideways, colliding with the unforgiving concrete wall. He crumpled, face first, onto cold, hard gravel. His back ached from the impact. He rose unsteadily to one knee. The ground rumbled and shook. Nashgrakh reached out for him, and John could sense his anticipation of victory, apparently uninterested in the rising din.

A blindingly bright light drenched them both. Nashgrakh looked up in surprise, and John leaped with all his might, shoving him backwards. John scrambled back and pressed flat against the tunnel wall.

A loud horn blared, and the train smashed into Nashgrakh. He went under the wheels.

John tried not to move as the train whooshed past. His clothes fluttered in the wind of its passage.

Brakes squealed, echoing deafeningly. His ears rang in pain.

The train took a long time to screech to a stop.

John needed to make himself scarce before anyone else entered the tunnel, but he had unfinished business first. In the dim light, John followed the sense of foreboding darkness and found Nashgrakh's mangled body. The creature wasn't dead. John felt the dark spark of its essence.

Kill!

Without knowing why, John pushed the ring against Nashgrakh's body. The creature made a gurgling groan.

Consume!

John willed Nashgrakh's essence into himself.

Strength surged within him, and he felt more powerful than ever. The darkness was gone. Nashgrakh was dead, leaving behind the husk of a broken and mangled human corpse.

John followed Jessica's presence to the crowd near the stopped train. He marched briskly to her.

"Let's go," he said quietly. "The train's no longer an option."

She opened her mouth and then looked around. *"Chuyện gì đã xảy ra thế?"* she asked.

"I'll explain later," he said. "We have to go before the police arrive."

They made their way through the city streets, away from the sirens, and stopped near a payphone. Jessica caught her breath. John didn't need to.

"Nashgrakh?" she asked.

"Dead," John said.

"Oh," Jessica said. "Good, right?"

Power surged through his veins. "Very good. He caught a train."

"Oh," she said thoughtfully. "The poor driver."

Nothing I do is ever good enough!

"If I hadn't done that, Nashgrakh would have killed me, killed you, and destroyed the world!"

Jessica was quiet for a while. "I wasn't criticising you. I just feel bad for him."

A twinge of something that might have been guilt flickered in John's mind but was quickly drowned out by the power coursing through him. He rubbed his temple and then pointed to the booth. "Payphone."

"Thank you." Jessica looked at him, her eyebrows raised. "I'm surprised you remembered." Her voice carried a hint of bitterness.

He waved off her thanks, sincere or not, and focused on the feelings of power within. He felt like he could take on anything; he never wanted to feel helpless again.

Jessica said something, but he didn't hear.

"What?"

"I said do you have any coins? For the payphone."

"Oh, right," he said and searched his pocket.

"Are you all right, miss? Is this man bothering you?" said a man from behind them. He looked to be in his late thirties, dressed in a sharp suit and tie, his hair neatly styled. Human, not ethereal.

"We're fine here, thanks," John said in a biting tone.

The men faced off against each other.

"I was talking to the lady, thank you very much."

"It's okay, really," Jessica said. "I was just going to use the payphone to call my parents." She looked pleadingly at John. "Bình tĩnh."

"What's that?" the stranger asked. "Why don't you come with me? How about we just—"

Hit him!

John snarled and punched the man in the gut. He flew backwards and collapsed on the ground like a ragdoll. Injured or dead, John didn't know and didn't particularly care.

"What the hell are you doing?" Jessica screamed in a high-pitched voice.

"He was going to cause problems," John responded coldly.

"He was trying to help!"

"He was trying to help *you*. He was going to call the police on me."

"So what?" She had tears in her eyes.

"If he called the police, best-case scenario is that I'd be arrested,"

She rolled her eyes. "Arrested?"

"And worst-case scenario, I'd end up dead."

"Dead? You're insane."

His eyes flashed with anger. "Don't be so goddamned naïve."

Had she never seen the news? Read a newspaper? Had any idea of life outside her parents' ivory tower?

They glared at each other, ignoring the unconscious man on the ground.

"Do you seriously not get that being Black is a health hazard when dealing with the police? You're too smart to be so ignorant.

The police might be your friend, but they'll never be mine. When they see me, they see a Black thug who should be behind bars. When they see you, they see a smart Asian girl who deserves the benefit of the doubt. They'd handle you with kid gloves but think I'm a dangerous threat and use force accordingly."

Jessica rolled her eyes and walked away to check on the interfering stranger.

"He's breathing but unconscious," she reported.

John looked around. He couldn't see or hear anyone, or sense any ethereal presence.

John seethed with rage and fury that she would so willingly invalidate his and other Black people's experiences. John clenched his fists and paced back and forth, his footsteps loud on the concrete beneath him.

When he looked over, Jessica was on her feet. She'd repositioned the man onto his side with an arm outstretched and head tilted back. John didn't understand why but didn't care.

She walked over to the payphone.

"Don't you need coins?" he asked.

"No. I'm calling an ambulance, arsehole."

"Fine, be that way."

He rummaged through the stranger's pockets and found a set of keys with a BMW logo. Jessica was still on the payphone, but he didn't care to listen to the details.

The keys had a fob with buttons.

Fancy.

John pushed the button with an open padlock symbol. There was a high-pitched *bip bip*, and a car on the side of the road flashed its headlights. He headed towards it.

It was a black BMW with only two doors. The badge on the back read, "318i." He had no idea what that meant, but he knew that BMWs were expensive.

"What are you doing?" Jessica asked. She sounded horrified.

"It's not enough you've nearly killed him, you want to steal his car, too?"

John had no patience left for this bullshit. "Unless you want to die, we're taking this car."

The standoff lasted a second.

Jessica said, "Give me the keys."

"Why?" he asked.

"Do you know how to drive?"

He threw the keys to her, and she snatched them out of the air. It was a good point. He'd never had the opportunity or money for lessons.

They climbed into the car.

Jessica clicked in her seatbelt, started the engine, and looked at him expectantly.

"Put the seatbelt on," she said.

"No," he said.

"If we crash—"

"I have a magic ring that will magically heal me, so I'm fine, thanks."

She looked pissed off.

"You're wasting valuable time right now," he said.

She shook her head but put the car in gear and pulled onto the road.

CHAPTER TEN

John looked at the street signs as Jessica drove.

"Get back across the river, then head west," he said.

She grunted an acknowledgement as she changed gears and lifted her foot off the clutch. The wail of sirens called somewhere behind them. John looked around, spooked.

"Hiding in the hotel didn't work. The ethereals just home in on you no matter where you are. We should head to Griffin's shack."

"Uh-huh," Jessica said.

He felt her frostiness but didn't care.

They drove in silence for several minutes.

Jessica was the first to speak. "So, end of the world, hey? Funny you didn't mention that earlier."

John grimaced. "I was hoping it wouldn't come up, actually."

"Why? Too unbelievable for me?"

"Well, yeah, of course. But Griffin might have been guessing about that bit."

"Might have?"

John shrugged. "Like I said earlier, he didn't tell me everything. There's a lot I don't know. He just said to find you and save you, and that's what I'm doing."

"Right," she said, abruptly businesslike. "So why Griffin's shack?"

"Because it's shielded against ethereal ... senses."

"How do you know that?"

"He lived there for decades with this ring, and the ethereals never bothered him. That's good enough for me."

"You and Griffin were close?"

"You could say that." John smiled sadly.

"How close?" She raised an eyebrow.

"Oh, Jesus, no! He was like two hundred years old!"

"Right, sorry, sorry. Was just wondering."

"Griffin was my only friend. He was like my ... like a kindly old uncle, or at least what I imagine one would be like." John sighed. "Let's take stock for a moment."

"Okay," Jessica said. She concentrated on the road ahead of her.

"I have no idea how many of these ethereals are after us."

"Great," Jessica said drily.

"Let's start with Nashgrakh."

"Crazy guy. Tried to kill me with a pole."

"That's the one." John laughed. "You bashed him in the face with a fucking tree. That was fucking awesome!"

Jessica gave a slight smile. "I aim to please."

"Anyway, he's dead. I made sure."

"I don't want to know the details," Jessica said with a squeamish expression.

"Who was next?"

"The shopping centre pair."

"Oh, yeah," he said. "Yekhtreshk."

"Young guy?"

"That's the one. I'm pretty sure he's dead. I think Zeluniel killed him."

"Such a shame," she said sarcastically.

"That leaves Zeluniel," he said.

"Old woman?"

"Yeah. She's the only light creature we've encountered. I haven't sensed her since the hotel." He gritted his teeth. "She seems stronger since she, uh, finished off Yekhtreshk."

"Well, that's not good," Jessica said calmly as if they were discussing bad weather. "And you have no idea how many there are?"

"It's one of the many, many things Griffin didn't have time to tell me."

"Hopefully, now we've got a car, we can put those troubles behind us, get a big head start, and hide out in your friend's hidey hole."

"Yeah," he said.

"That still leaves Yondarel. It sounds like an ethereal name, right?"

"Yeah, about that, I've got"—John stared at the upcoming overpass, sensing danger—"Watch out!"

She looked over at him, alarmed. "What do you—"

The roof of the car crumpled as something large and heavy fell on it. Then, a crazed-looking young woman landed on her hands and knees on the front of the car. Darkness like a starless night sky oozed from the ethereal, who John instinctively understood was Gralkrakh, and the hidden figure on the roof.

"Cover your eyes!" John yelled.

Jessica screamed and covered her eyes with one hand. The car swerved wildly, scraping against the kerb. She tried in vain to regain control, but the car continued its erratic course, narrowly missing a streetlight.

Gralkrakh, the dark ethereal crouched on the front of the car, punched through the windscreen. The pane of glass held together, and her bloodied hand caught. John touched her fist with the ring. Gralkrakh shrieked as her skin sizzled, falling backwards off the car and ripping out the entire windscreen.

A double thump confirmed she'd been run over by both sets of wheels. The car banked back and forth across the road, and John grabbed the steering wheel to keep it steady. He looked up and wondered where the other dark creature was.

A fist ripped through the metal roof and smashed into John's shoulder, shattering it. He let go of the wheel with a guttural grunt of agony. He closed his eyes and willed away the pain, gritting his teeth as his shoulder rebuilt itself.

The creature felt like the utter darkness of a deep mine shaft, and he instinctually knew its name was Zhelktrakh.

John's face was a mask of rage. He planted his feet firmly on the seat, crouched down as much as the confined space would allow, and then propelled himself upwards. With both hands, he smashed into the roof, tearing it open like a tin can. Zhelktrakh was flung into the air and off the road. The night felt brighter without the dark one with them.

"You can open your eyes now," John said.

Jessica did and groaned as she wrestled with the steering wheel. In the chaos of the fight, she'd taken her foot off the accelerator, and the car had slowed significantly. The engine groaned in protest, lurching as it struggled with the high gear at such a low speed. Jessica's hand darted to the gearstick, quickly changing gears. The car's grumbling ceased, settling into a smoother ride as it matched the lower speed.

However, the roof was bent back and acted like a sail, forcing the car to list uncontrollably. John stood and slowly bent the roof back into shape, making the tortured sound of twisting metal. It was roughly horizontal again but with a gaping hole in the middle and unsealed on the sides and front. It vibrated loudly, and air blew through the car with an obnoxious, piercing whistle.

The car was now a cacophony of vibrating metal and

whistling wind, but at least it was under control. John slumped back into his seat, spent. Out of the corner of his eye, Jessica gripped the steering wheel tightly. She kept stealing glances at him, her face a mix of shock and disbelief. The silence between them was heavy, and he could almost feel the weight of her unasked questions about his sudden display of strength.

"Oh no," John said in a subdued tone. Gralkrakh's dark presence was nearby. He looked through the mirrors. Where was she? "Don't slow down," he said.

Jessica grunted in response and sped up.

The driver's door ripped off and flew away. Gralkrakh gripped the edge of the now-exposed door frame and wedged her feet against the side of the car. With her free hand she clutched at Jessica's upper arm.

Jessica's seatbelt cut into her chest and stomach. Gralkrakh let go of the car and with both hands pulled on Jessica's legs with all her might. She held fast to the steering wheel, but her legs slipped off the pedals.

The car slowed and careened as Jessica's body was twisted and partially pulled out of the car.

John roared and leaped from the passenger seat into Jessica's lap, punching Gralkrakh square in the face. She screeched and flopped pathetically to the road, holding her burned face.

John pulled Jessica's legs back into the car and awkwardly removed himself from atop her skirt. Tears streamed down her face while she methodically worked her way back up through the gears.

John slowed his breathing so he could think clearly. It felt brighter in the car without the dark creatures, but inexplicably, he felt Zeluniel's blazing presence. The car must have slowed enough for Zeluniel to catch them on foot.

"You've got to be fucking kidding me," he muttered.

Jessica turned to him, distraught.

"Go faster, now!" John yelled

Zeluniel must be running behind them. John tried to get a read on which direction she would attack from and readied himself to fight.

The passenger door flew out into the night, and wiry, gnarled hands grabbed him. Before he could react, John was thrown from the car and smashed onto the asphalt road.

Chapter Eleven

John rolled to a stop, picking up extra scrapes and bruises, which healed as he jumped to his feet and prepared to fight back.

Zeluniel was slower. One of her ankles had snapped in the fall but clicked back into place as he watched.

John caught her off guard. He punched her temple, and she reeled but quickly returned with an uppercut to his chin. John retreated a few steps.

His ring had done nothing. It burned the dark creatures but not the light, apparently. John would have to beat her the old-fashioned way. He didn't have a great track record of success in fistfights. He also didn't have a choice.

John threw all his weight behind a powerful punch. Zeluniel easily stepped out of the way, grabbed his elbow, and used her other hand to slip the ring off his finger.

John spun around in a panic. Without the ring, he could no longer feel Jessica's presence. He considered running, but her escape was a higher priority.

He balled his fists and crouched low, ready to strike if Zeluniel came at him. Instead, she stood back and watched him calmly. Patiently.

His head throbbed as if he'd been punched.

His eyebrow and lip tore back open and bled.

His body ached, and he struggled to breathe.

His vision blurred, and his shoulders slumped.

Zeluniel watched and waited. John understood her patience now. She didn't have to do anything to beat him except wait.

Cuts opened on his arms and neck, and his forearm re-broke. He wheezed, unable to breathe as if strangled by an invisible hand. His shoulder dislocated, the bones shattering into fragments beneath his skin. He tried to back away, but his ankle snapped, and he fell to the ground. John screamed at the pain. He tried and failed to crawl away. His knuckles broke; his fingers fractured.

He cried into the asphalt in more pain than he'd ever experienced in his nineteen years. Ragged breaths came painfully.

Once he was immobilised, Zeluniel approached and inspected him carefully. He couldn't sense her brightness anymore, but she stood so close he could smell the sour, musty odour of her breath.

All was still for several seconds.

Then she grabbed him by his unbroken ankle and dragged him off the road and along the gravel.

John flailed and screamed, but it achieved nothing except steal his breath.

He cried uncontrollably, torn between wishing that Jessica would return to save him and being thankful she'd escaped.

It wasn't long before he blacked out, a trail of blood in his wake.

John opened his eyes in the darkness, free of pain. Moonlight spilled in through the window, casting a milky light over the room. It was a simple, high-ceilinged space. The dim light revealed shelves lining the walls, some holding bats and balls. The scent of rubber and leather hung in the air, indicating this was a sports equipment shed. He couldn't see anyone but wasn't alone. He felt a sensation akin to bright, raking lights on his skin. He tentatively tried to move but was restrained, the hard back of the chair pressing against him.

The old woman stepped into view. Zeluniel. Her essence shone like a lighthouse. John forced himself not to shy away. He glared at her and said nothing. Griffin's warning that they would understand his intent if he spoke echoed in his mind.

She watched him carefully, her stillness unnerving, like a predator poised to strike. There was no beauty in her statue-like immobility, only a chilling sense of danger.

He realised he was in no pain. His wounds were all healed. Moving only his eyes, he looked down and saw Larulia, a light creature he'd not encountered before, holding a ring to his skin. Her presence burned hot and bright like an incandescent bulb. There was a third presence in the room, hidden behind him. Bright too, but cold and aloof like a distant star.

Zeluniel spoke. "Where is the girl?"

He declined to answer.

"Where is the girl?"

Still, he refused.

She looked at Larulia. "Remove Yondarel."

Larulia stepped back. Immediately the sensation of overwhelming brightness left him, and the room felt darker. He could no longer *feel* the ethereals.

Invisible punches wracked his head and body. His injuries returned in full force, each cut and fracture a fresh source of agony. He tried to stare her down, but his body betrayed him. His breath came in ragged gasps, and his shoulders slumped forwards as much as the restraints would allow.

John focused on the old woman's wrinkled features, trying to still his thoughts. Sweat trickled down his face, mingling with the blood from his reopened wounds. His body felt cold and distant, as if he was floating away from the pain. His shoulder popped out of its socket, and he cried out. He quickly bit down on the scream, focusing on the crow's feet next to her eyes.

His body continued to fail. His fists clenched involuntarily, bones grinding against each other. He sobbed, but kept his gaze fixed on the ethereal before him. He wouldn't let his mind wander, wouldn't give her the satisfaction of seeing him break. He focused on the here and now, on the pain and the ethereal causing it. He wouldn't think of anyone else, wouldn't risk giving anything away. He had to endure, for Jessica's sake.

He glared at her until his head dropped, and dizziness and blackness consumed him.

John didn't know how many times they repeated the cycle of torment with the ring. He couldn't keep track.

Zeluniel's hideous visage loomed as she leaned in to inspect him. Her presence was blindingly bright.

"Tell me where the girl is, or I will rip you apart, limb by limb."

His gaze met hers, a silent defiance in his eyes. His body trembled, torn between the urge to protect Jessica and the desperate need for the pain to cease. He tried not to whimper.

"Killing you would take no effort."

He knew she was telling the truth.

"If you do not help me, I will kill you and use your body to find her."

John's mouth was dry. He could feel that this wasn't an empty threat. He squeezed his lips together and didn't make a sound.

"One way or another, you will help me find her. Will you do it alive or dead? This is your final chance. Tell me where she is."

He ignored her once again, and the ring was pulled away. The room seemed to darken, now unable to feel the bright presence of the light ethereals. John's body convulsed as the familiar pain returned, the bruises on his face blooming once more. The relentless cycle of healing and hurting was a torment in itself, a predictable drip, drip, drip of agony.

This time, Zeluniel did something different. She gripped his left arm, her fingers digging into his flesh. Planting her foot against his chest for leverage, she pulled with a force that seemed inhuman. His muscles, tendons, and joints strained against the pressure, but they couldn't hold. With a sound that would haunt his nightmares, his arm was torn from his body. He screamed, a raw, primal sound, and then the blackness took him.

Zeluniel looked pleased.

John's laughter echoed in his head, a wild, unhinged sound that didn't feel like his own. Zeleniel had torn off both of his arms. He twitched his fingers. Both arms were back in place for now. She'd obviously put the ring back on to restore his health. But why did she look so pleased? Her gaze was a bright beacon, piercing into his very soul. He felt exposed, laid bare before her, his thoughts spiralling into a chaotic whirl.

"I know where the girl is going," Zeluniel said.

John felt for the intention beyond her words. He sensed … untruth. The ethereal was *lying* to him. A jolt of surprise shot through him. Zeluniel knew what suburb Jessica was heading to, but no more than that.

"Her name is Jessica Brown," she continued.

John tried not to reply.

"Your name is John Wedgewood."

John tried not to panic.

"Your friend, the killer, was Griffin Pembroke."

These weren't questions; she was just stating facts. How

much had he revealed in his delirious stupor? Did she know everything?

No. She'd have let me die if she knew everything.

She still needed something. He wondered what. He tried to think indirectly about the problem, careful not to let any intentions slip out in a sound or a word. It was hard to concentrate in the presence of the three beings. Their essences reached out and overwhelmed him with brightness. As he struggled to maintain his mental composure, a thought occurred to him. During the *ordeal*, his mind had been a whirlwind of pain and fear, too chaotic for any clear intentions to be read. Hopefully? Now, he needed to replicate that chaos, to cloud his thoughts and keep his plans hidden.

If Jessica had made it to the shack, the lead walls should prevent the creatures from finding her. Jessica might still be safe, even if they knew her approximate location.

Zeluniel's radiance flickered, the brightness dimming ever so slightly. John interpreted this as a sign of her displeasure at his newfound confidence and assurance.

Zeluniel addressed her accomplices. "Go ahead of me and start searching the area. I will let him die, take his body, and join the hunt soon."

She said this while the ring was against his body, and John knew she spoke the truth; she wanted him to know.

Zeluniel leered at him, her lips pulling back in a grotesque smile that revealed jagged, yellowed teeth. Her eyes, cold and devoid of any human warmth, bore into him with a chilling intensity. A wave of terror washed over him; his heart pounded in his chest. It struck a deep, instinctual chord of fear within him.

"Farewell," Zeluniel said as Larulia left the room.

The incandescent sensation left with Larulia. John spied the third creature, Unrelya, as she walked in front of him to leave. The sensation of cold aloofness dimmed as she left.

Zeluniel removed the ring and placed it out of view. The room seemed to darken again, and John's body started the long, slow, and painful process of breaking down, one injury at a time.

He cried uncontrollably. It was so cold. He'd failed Jessica. He'd failed Griffin. He'd failed everyone. The world was going to end, and it was John Wedgewood's fault.

CHAPTER TWELVE

He heard a commotion outside. In his delirious state, the sounds of a fight, angry roars and screams were surreal.

It was dark, and he could barely see, but someone was in the room with him. A young Asian woman in an oversized leather jacket, concerned and emotional, like she cared for him deeply. He should tell her he wasn't into girls. He didn't want to lead her on.

"John?" she asked.

Who was that? He didn't know.

In the dim light, the young woman moved closer to him, her face etched with worry. She kneeled beside him, her oversized leather jacket rustling softly in the quiet room.

A warm sensation spread through his body, like a rush of life-giving energy. He glanced down to see the woman pressing something golden against his skin. She then reached for something on the ground, her arm straining slightly under its weight. It was his detached arm, he realised with a start.

A strange sensation prickled at his side, a tingling that quickly escalated into a sharp, intense pain. It was agonising, yet oddly familiar, like the pins and needles of a limb waking up after losing blood circulation. But this was more intense, more immediate. He gasped—he could feel his arm again. It was reattached, healing at an astonishing rate.

A wild panic increased in tenor, as if the volume were being turned up. An inaudible background wail: Yondarel was alarmed.

John jerked with alertness as his faculties returned to him. His bindings were gone, and he could feel Jessica's presence again.

"Shh!" Jessica hushed him. She held a human arm—his right arm!—to his shoulder. The tendons, sinews, muscles, and skin stitched themselves together.

"Barcelona," he croaked out.

Jessica laughed, and her eyes welled up with tears.

He felt whole. He felt strong.

He felt … fucking livid.

"Where is she?" he growled.

Jessica's lips curled into a faint smile, her eyes gleaming with a hint of smug satisfaction. "They're fighting outside."

"Who?" he asked.

"The ethereals that jumped on the car and the ones that were already here."

He took a moment to put the pieces together.

"You led them here?"

"Yes." Jessica's smug satisfaction deepened, her eyes sparkling with a newfound confidence. A lopsided smile, bold and unapologetic, tugged at the corner of her mouth.

He grabbed her in a bear hug. "That's fucking genius! But you should be hidden! Why are you here?"

She looked at him with a stern expression. "I wasn't going to let them kill you."

A lump formed in his throat, and warmth spread through his chest. He blinked back unexpected tears. No one had ever risked so much for him, not even the person who had named him.

"You are insane. And awesome." He smiled genuinely. "What's the plan?"

She straightened her back, meeting his gaze head-on. "I drove the car up to the building and bailed out, led the creatures here, and they started fighting. I figured we could run to the car while they're distracted and get out of here before they've noticed we've escaped."

"Sounds like a plan," he said. "Let's go!"

The scene outside was fantastical.

Backlit by headlights, two melees were being fought. Larulia and Unrelya grappled a dark ethereal. It was Gralkrakh who kept them both at bay. It felt like twin piercing beams clashing with a starless night.

Zeluniel gloated at Zhelktrakh, who snarled and backed away from her ring. That battle felt like a lighthouse fighting a deep, dark mine shaft.

Jessica sprinted for the car. She'd left the engine idling, ready to go. The front doors and windscreen were missing, but the BMW badge held on.

Don't flee. Kill.

John felt possessed. He marched over to Zeluniel with no fear. She brought her arm back to punch Zhelktrakh, and John grabbed her elbow. She turned her head towards him in surprise.

John now understood instinctively that the body before him was merely a suit worn by a malevolent, formless being. Instead of the old woman's body, he now saw within to the ageless, genderless, malevolent being of light. His true enemy.

Kill!

John ripped the ring—the anchor named Ludalya—off Zeluniel's finger and threw it at Zhelktrakh, who screamed as it connected. With a savage wrench, John snapped the neck of Zeluniel's body, releasing the ethereal essence.

Zeluniel had thought Griffin a killer. Now John was, too. No regrets.

Consume!

John sensed Zeluniel's freed essence before him and willed it into himself.

His entire being pulsed with power, and he slammed the ground with his fist. The four remaining ethereals lost their footing, blasted off their feet by an invisible wave. John advanced and growled in frustration as they scrambled to their feet and retreated at speed in different directions. He lunged forward, aching for the chase, but they'd already scattered. The taste of victory bittersweet, he wanted *more*.

"John!"

He looked over. Jessica called out to him.

"Let's go!"

Her request snapped him out of his altered state. Getting to safety was more important than hunting ethereals. He jogged to the car and climbed in.

"Quickly," Jessica said. "And put on—"

He clipped in his seat belt.

"—your seatbelt."

She gave him a wry smile, put the car into gear, and gunned the engine.

It was not a quiet ride.

The wind blasted through the open car, and the roof rattled and whistled. They couldn't go as fast as they liked, but it was quicker than running.

John was silent. He stared into the night's darkness and noticed the moon was higher than before. The wind whipped at him viciously, and he was consumed by hysterical laughter that soon turned into sobs and wails.

Jessica clenched her teeth and gripped the steering wheel tighter.

John fell silent again, his face hot with tears.

Boys don't cry? That adage no longer applied. After what he'd experienced, he didn't think he'd be able to hold it in again. He'd promised not to fall apart until after saving Jessica, but now all bets were off.

John looked over at Jessica. She was barefaced and raw, covered with blood—probably his—her hair blown about by the wind. She still wore his leather jacket.

"Jessica," he said.

"Yes, John."

"You are the bravest girl I've ever … No, that sounds insulting. Bravest lady?"

"Woman," she offered.

"The bravest woman I've ever met. Thank you for saving me."

Tears streamed down her face. "You're very welcome, John."

It had been a hell of a night.

When Griffin died, John thought he'd be forever friendless. Perhaps, if they both survived and the world didn't end, he'd have a new friend.

"Oh, I almost forgot," John said. "Where are my manners?"

Jessica looked at him with a confused expression.

"I haven't properly introduced you. How rude of me." He held up his hand with the ring. "Yondarel, this is Jessica Brown. Jessica, Yondarel."

Her eyes widened.

"Yeah, this little bastard is one of *them*. A light creature, or the essence of one anyway, shoved into a metal casing. All of those creatures we saw tonight are basically wearing people-suits. The dark creatures hunt and consume to power the bodies, but the light ones use these rings. I suppose using one of their own as a power source beats having to keep hunting people." He shrugged.

"Is it … safe to have around?" she asked nervously.

"Hell if I know," John said flippantly. "But given how much they fucked me up in there, I think I'll keep hold of this little life support bastard for the rest of my life. Even if it is the enemy."

They fell into an uneasy silence. They left the city, travelled through the quiet suburbs, through darkness punctuated by the occasional streetlight, and hoped not to pass any police cars.

They drove slowly along the residential street, past where John had had the snot beaten out of him earlier in the day. That was paradise compared to what he'd just been through.

He noticed the bike was still there. He was surprised it hadn't been stolen yet.

He pointed to the park, and Jessica pulled up next to the old shack. He hoped no one called the police. A BMW parked next to a shack in a park in the middle of the night, its roof held on by a thread, and missing a windscreen and two doors, was clearly stolen. He hoped the Griffin Tree Row would shield it from view.

John stepped out of the car. It felt weird not having to open the door first. He told Jessica to hang back for a moment and walked to where he'd last spoken to Griffin.

"I did it, my friend. I stopped them from getting her."

He stared at nothing for a few moments and felt suddenly self-conscious. "I mean, I had some help, but nobody's perfect, right?"

Feeling foolish, he walked back to Jessica and led her to the shack. John realised it looked like a haphazard assembly of lopsided rusted corrugated iron and felt self-conscious. She eyed it with suspicion. "Your friend lived in *that?*"

John bristled. "Yes, for more than half a century, and he seemed pretty happy with it, and it's withstood storms and the test of time. Let's head in."

The screech of the metal door admitted entry to the small dwelling.

John pulled out his lighter—his ethereal interrogators hadn't bothered to empty his pockets—and lit it. The flickering flame cast long, dancing shadows across the interior, revealing the uncluttered space where Griffin had lived for decades. A single table, a chair, and a bed filled most of the space. The walls, made of corrugated iron, were bare.

"Wait here a moment," he said.

"Sure thing."

John could sense Jessica was more than happy not to enter yet.

John rummaged around the cluttered table until his fingers closed around the familiar shape of a candle. He placed it on the table and lit it, the warm glow pushing back the shadows. He waved her in, shutting the corrugated iron door behind her with a metallic screech.

"Well, we're here," he said. "We should be safe for now."

CHAPTER THIRTEEN

Jessica placed the car keys on the table and looked around with a horrified expression. "How exactly is this place supposed to keep me hidden?"

"Oh. The uh, walls are lined with lead."

"Lead!"

"Shh! Keep it down. If anyone calls the cops, we're in deep shit."

She buried her head in her hands. "Okay, I'll just not touch the walls then."

"Probably a good idea."

"How exactly did he get so much lead?" She looked around uneasily. "You'd think the government would object to it in a park."

John scratched his neck. "I'm not sure they know about it, to be honest. As for where, he said an old mine nearby at Mount C—"

"Oh!" she said excitedly, "I know that one!"

"You do? I'd never heard of it before."

"Yeah, it's a local mystery. I read about it a lot in high school. I … did a lot of reading in high school." She looked self-conscious.

"It must be an old mystery, then. Griffin said it happened about sixty years ago."

Jessica nodded. "A dozen men died, but there was no record of them ever working there."

"Weird," John said. "Could the company have destroyed records to avoid compensation or something?"

"It's possible. But if I'm remembering correctly, no family members came forward. It's like the workers had never existed."

"How did they die?"

"A gas leak was the leading theory, but it was never proven. That's why it's still unsolved. There were signs of a struggle, and the victims had scrapes and bruises but no injuries that could have caused death. No gas leaks were detected, but the powers that be decided it was just safer to shut the place down and stop anyone from going there."

"The company didn't object to closing it down?"

Jessica shrugged. "Maybe. I'm not sure. But governments haven't always been beholden to corporate interests. Sometimes they'd shut down or break up businesses acting against the public good."

"I can't imagine what that must be like," John said.

She shrugged again. "Times change, you know? 'Greed is good' and all that."

"Yeah, because the greediest people are always the nicest," John drily remarked.

Jessica smiled in response.

"Do you know where the mine is?" John asked.

"I think there's an old dirt path off one of the main roads up the hill. There are probably 'stay away'-type signs."

"Should we keep it as a backup location?"

"In case of emergency?"

"Yeah. If the creatures find us here, we have somewhere else to go. It might not be fully mined out, so there could be enough lead to keep you hidden."

"You're not worried about gas leaks?"

He shrugged. "It's a backup. I don't really want to hide in an abandoned mine in the middle of nowhere. But also"—he moved his hands up and down like balancing scales—"die of gas poisoning or killed by monsters and bring about the end of the world?"

She shuddered. "Not much of a choice, really."

"No," John said darkly. He thought of his treatment earlier in the night. "But not a difficult one for me."

Silence. Jessica looked around the shack.

"I don't suppose there's a phone in here?"

"No," John said, "it's pretty basic. Candles are pretty much the most advanced technology here other than, you know, doors, walls, and a roof."

"I don't know if I could live like this."

"I said something similar, too, years ago."

"And?"

John laughed gently. "Griffin said, 'People did live perfectly fine before electricity, my dear boy.' And since he was over two hundred years old, he spoke from experience."

"I can't imagine living for so long, seeing so many changes in society."

"Seeing everyone you care about die," John added soberly.

He looked at the floor. Being in Griffin's shack without him made his death all the more real.

"I didn't mean to bring the mood down."

"No, it's"—her eyes widened—"Wait, what did he eat?"

"What?"

"There's no fridge. No cupboard or tins or bottles or anything. No toilet! What did this man eat and drink?"

John sat in silence.

"You know, I never did see him eat," he said thoughtfully. "Isn't that funny? The whole time I knew him, I never saw him eat or drink or even take a shit."

"What did you do when you were here?"

John shrugged. "I never ate or drank here. As for Griffin, I guess I never really thought about it. I started coming here when I was really young, and kids don't think about that. It was just normal for Griffin's place. He was always a bit of a mystery in so many ways. And the absence of a toilet is something boys can deal with easily."

Jessica's face showed her disgust.

"Yeah, yeah." He waved off her reaction.

"It might have been decades since he last had a meal," she said thoughtfully.

"Or centuries if his possession of Yondarel is what we're going by."

Jessica eyed the ring suspiciously.

"One of the last things he told me," John said, his voice thick with emotion, "was that he couldn't remember the last time he'd been sick or hurt. And that he'd been alive for too long and would have lost his humanity without my friendship."

He couldn't continue. His chest ached at the loss of his friend, and he allowed silent tears to stream down his face.

On some level, John had assumed that getting Jessica to safety would get his life back to normal. But it wouldn't. It couldn't. Griffin was dead and never coming back.

Jessica spoke, and she did so quietly. "John, I want to tell you something."

John wiped his face on his sleeve. "Yeah?"

"I wasn't entirely honest with you earlier."

John forced himself to lighten up. He put his hand on his chest and dramatically intoned, "Don't tell me Barcelona was a lie! I couldn't bear to live."

She rolled her eyes and shook her head. "I would never lie about such a thing!" she said in mock horror. Then the smile left her face, and she looked nervous. Vulnerable.

"I told you I was too busy for relationships, and you said I was using that as an excuse."

"Ah, yes. I did say that." He looked sheepish.

"The thing is …" She looked at the floor. "You weren't too far off the mark."

"Really?" he said, surprised. "I thought I was just being an arsehole."

"Oh, you were, but you weren't completely wrong."

"In what way?"

"I've never had any interest in relationships. Romantic or sexual. I love my family. I love my friends. But romantic or sexual feelings? I just … don't have them."

"You just haven't found the right person yet," John said. "You're young."

She looked frustrated like she was trying to explain microbiology to a toddler. "That's what everyone says, but it's not like that. I'm not going to wake up one day and 'grow up.' I'm not immature just because I don't want to have sex. This is me."

He didn't know how to respond.

She stared sadly at the floor. "I thought you, of all people, might understand."

"What do you mean?"

She gave him a hard expression. "How likely are you to wake up one day and decide to settle down with a nice girl?"

He began to respond but stopped himself and thought back to his assumption that she used makeup to appeal to men.

After a few thoughtful moments, he simply said, "I'm sorry."

Her expression softened.

"I don't understand how you feel," John said, "but almost nobody understands my feelings, either. Or that I am how I am by nature and not by choice. I'm sorry I did to you what everyone else does to me."

"Thank you, John," she whispered, tears in her eyes.

"My life has been shit, but I understand now that it doesn't mean other people have it easy. It's not a competition." John shifted uncomfortably. "I'm going for a smoke. Back in a sec."

She gave him a knowing look, but he pointed to the ring.

"I'm immortal, remember? Cancer can't touch me!"

She rolled her eyes. "Knock yourself out."

He stepped outside and closed the rickety door behind him. The moon was hidden behind clouds, and he felt a few spits of rain. He should have finished his cigarette by the time the downpour hit in earnest.

Jessica was safe, but would she have to live here forever? Trapped in the shack like a caged animal? Was he supposed to bring her food and drink until she died of old age? He could barely afford to feed himself.

It could wait until tomorrow; they'd been through too much tonight.

John rolled a cigarette, lit it, and inhaled.

Something felt off. He smoked for a bit longer and then looked at the cigarette in betrayal. It wasn't doing anything for him.

Disgusted, he threw the cigarette down and stamped it out with his foot.

Well, fuck. Guess I'm a non-smoker now.

He turned back to the shack as the rain increased, then froze.

He'd shut the door. The lead-lined door in the lead-lined shack.

So why could he still feel Jessica's presence?

Chapter Fourteen

John rushed into the shack.

Jessica sat upright and let out a sharp, battle-ready cry, her fists swinging wildly.

He closed the screeching door carefully behind him. "It's okay! It's just—Barcelona!"

Jessica's eyes focused on him, her tense posture relaxing into exhaustion.

"Sorry, I must have drifted off." She ran her hand down her face. "Is it morning yet?"

"No, I was only outside for a few minutes."

"Oh." She looked confused. "All the running and hiding must have taken it out of me."

She grimaced and prodded her chest and abdomen where the seatbelt had bruised her.

"We've got a problem," John said.

"Okay, I'm listening," she said.

"I can feel your presence from outside the shack."

He waited for her to understand the implication.

"Oh!" She looked concerned. "How?"

"The lead dampens it a lot, but not entirely. It's less distinct than when you're in the open or a building, but there it is."

"What do you think we should do?"

"I might be overreacting. Unless an ethereal walks through this particular park, we're probably alright. And if not, we have the car and the lead mine to fall back to. I don't think they'll be able to feel your presence from longer distances. I just thought it would mask you completely. Griffin must have thought that, too."

"Should we try to find the mine now?"

"It's night and raining. The mountain road might be dangerous as well. And even if we do get to the mine, we don't know what state it'll be in. And, of course, as soon as we leave the shack, the ethereals will be able to home in on you. We should keep the travel and search time to a minimum. Unless we get any unwanted visitors, we stay here where it's dry and the walls provide some protection. What do you think?"

She nodded sleepily. "It's probably for the best. I don't know about you, but I normally sleep through the night and am absolutely wrecked."

John didn't feel tired at all. Yondarel must be taking care of that.

"Alright, so that's our plan," John said. "We head up the mountain at dawn and look for the mine."

"Are you hungry at all? I'm starving."

"Yes," John said. He longed to consume.

"When was the last time you ate?"

"Food? Oh, I don't know, probably lunchtime."

She frowned. "Yes, food. What did you think I meant?"

"I, uh, thought you meant essences."

"Essences?"

"Ethereal essences, the creatures' real forms."

"I don't understand."

He thought about how to put this in as non-threatening a way as possible.

"When I made sure Nashgrakh was properly dead, I seemed to absorb his essence. Or Yondarel channelled it into me, or something. I don't know. It just happened."

"That's creepy, but it was an accident, right? So, no harm, no foul?"

"The thing is, it made me feel really, really strong. Stronger than ever. And ... I *liked* it."

She frowned, her brows knitting together. "That doesn't sound safe, John."

"There's more," he said, staring into the candle flame. "When I killed Zeluniel's host body, I consumed her essence too. Deliberately."

Jessica's expression turned ashen, and she recoiled.

"It made me powerful. I was able to knock the rest of the ethereals off their feet just by bashing the ground."

"It sounds like you're trying to justify it."

He shifted uncomfortably. "It's not like that. It's a good thing, right? I can better protect you if I'm stronger."

She stared at him for a long time.

"Thank you for sharing that with me," she said eventually. "I know being open with people is difficult, and I'm glad you trust me."

He breathed a sigh of relief and decided to leave it with her. They could always talk more later.

"You know, before all this happened," Jessica said, "the stresses in my life—school, work, my mother—seemed so important and overwhelming. Now that I've experienced actual danger, I wonder if such mundane things will bother me anymore. If nothing else, it's given me a perspective I lacked before."

John saw the dark circles under her eyes and how her shoulders were hunched.

"Alright, that's enough deep and meaningful conversation for one night. Off to sleep with you," he said. "You've got to drive in the morning, so get some rest. I'll stay awake and stand guard."

Jessica smiled at him. "Thank you, John. I'm glad you found me when you did."

"So am I," he said with a smile.

John moved the candle to the far corner of the table. Its glow lit the space but was dark enough that Jessica should be able to get some sleep.

The harsh rain rattled the metal roof.

Shit, the car! It'll be soaked by morning. Something to look forward to …

Sitting at Griffin's desk made John think about his old friend. His lack of hunger reminded him of what Jessica had said about her lack of appetite for romance and sex. It wasn't the same, of course, but it gave him a framework to try to understand it better.

He wondered about Griffin's past. Did he have friends, family, or loved ones? Maybe centuries ago, he did, back wherever he came from. The whole time they'd been friends, he'd never known him to have visitors, other friends, or partners. Griffin and Jessica had something in common, after all. He wondered how they would have got along. Or if they even would have. He smiled sadly.

A collection of old, yellowed papers covered in cursive hand-writing lay on the desk.

This must be Griffin's diary or something.

He wondered what a two-hundred-year-old immortal would have written down.

No, these were his private notes. He should respect his privacy, even though he was gone. Even more so since he wasn't around to stop anyone from looking.

John hesitated. Maybe he'd written about the ethereals hoping John would read it after rescuing Jessica?

If important information was in these notes and he didn't read them, he would be an idiot of the highest magnitude.

The rain intensified, hammering against the roof, and John started to read.

CHAPTER FIFTEEN

The papers weren't in any coherent order, but John managed to learn a little more about the ethereals.

He had already worked out that every light creature was actually two: the one who inhabited the dead body and the one who inhabited the anchor-ring. But from Griffin's investigations, he now understood the grizzly truth of how the dark creatures anchored themselves without rings. They killed people and absorbed their essence.

He had no idea what an essence actually was, however. Was it some kind of personal energy that runs the body? A soul? Regardless, the dark creatures didn't sacrifice any of their number to produce anchors. They instead needed to refuel over time to keep their stolen bodies.

John looked up from the notes and stared at the wall, eyes unfocused, as a thought came to him.

What had become of Ludalya, Zeluniel's anchor-ring? He'd thrown it at a dark creature but hadn't kept track of it afterwards. He could return for it once Jessica was safe in the mine; except he had no idea where the fight had happened. Hopefully Jessica knew. Something to ask her in the morning.

So far, he hadn't found any information about a person, a human person, absorbing ethereal essences. He idly wondered if Nashgrakh and Zeluniel lived on inside him.

Where did they get their bodies? Did they raid graveyards? Morgues? Did they hunt people down and collect bodies themselves directly by killing people? He wondered how many stories of missing persons, unexplained accidents, or unsolved murders over the centuries were, in fact, horrific encounters with dark creatures.

He felt sick. Griffin wasn't exaggerating when he'd called them a pestilence. And they'd been around for thousands of years. How much folklore and unexplained phenomena were ethereals operating in the world?

Griffin's writings also confirmed what John had suspected: the ethereal creatures, light and dark, could consume each other's essences after besting them in battle. He could safely chalk Yekhtreshk's fate up to that.

Zeluniel absorbed Yekhtreshk, and John absorbed Zeluniel, so did that mean he'd consumed both of them? Was he even entirely human anymore? He rubbed his temples. All these thoughts were doing his head in.

John skimmed over the detailed descriptions of ethereal battles in their ethereal realm. He knew the basics from the old stories Griffin used to tell him. The descriptions in the writing were more detailed and didn't stick with the conceit that they were just legends.

Vast hosts of ethereals would meet in glorious battle but never won the war as each side maintained a natural advantage in their own territory. Why they were warring in the first place was unclear to him. It could be something fundamental in their nature, or maybe their motivations were beyond human understanding. He wondered how Griffin had known, then glanced at Yondarel on his finger. Ah, like that. He must have taken that information from Yondarel somehow.

The most recent account from Griffin's papers was of a local widower in 1982, confronted by the return of his dead wife. That poor bastard. John realised how fortunate it was Griffin hadn't left a body behind. The thought of an ethereal possessing his body made him sick to the stomach.

John found himself engrossed in a recount of Griffin's travels. Griffin hadn't been a solitary wanderer: he led a group of men at least a century ago, something like an ethereal hunting or monitoring group. This was such a difference from the lone, reclusive hermit John had known him as.

The notes unveiled that the ethereal allure linked to Jessica was detected long before her birth. This raised a multitude of questions in John's mind. Was it her parents, grandparents, or even more distant forebears who had first emitted the call? If it was a family trait, that could explain the difficulties Griffin and the ethereals faced in pinpointing her. If her signal was being replicated in multiple locations—and across different countries —it would have been akin to trying to locate the origin of a sound in an echo chamber.

Griffin's notes documented how the siren call in his homeland abruptly weakened. He and his band of twelve had embarked on the RMS *Ophir* at London in 1907, securing passage in the ship's second class berths. They traced the path of the ethereal allure across the sea, a voyage marked by ethereal encounters and evasions. It also explained that her signal became stronger and more concentrated over years and decades, then intensified around two decades ago. John wondered when Jessica's mother migrated here and if that coincided with the jump in signal strength.

Something must have happened tonight, as it was the first time the signal could be narrowed down to a single person.

He sat back in Griffin's chair. What would Griffin have done if John hadn't visited him when he had? Was John so predictable that he knew he would come? But what if John had decided to stay in, was sick, or had an odd job? Is that why Griffin was out walking when he was? Was he coming to John's place? Nash-grakh would've snatched up Jessica before he reached her. He felt a sensation of almost vertigo at how close they came to losing Jessica and, he guessed, the world.

It wasn't clear how killing Jessica was supposed to end the world. Maybe the notes would have more.

Griffin could track Jessica's ancestors' locations, but only to their continent or country, maybe. Even then, he could only track one of the family lines. And he didn't know which family or families he was tracking. The signal must have been very weak back then. John couldn't imagine following those bread-crumbs across the world in those days.

Since Griffin was only one man, he couldn't track down all the separate strands of signals and instead remained wherever he felt the signal getting stronger. Why was Jessica the unlucky one? Why not her children or grandchildren? Maybe she wouldn't have children. Nothing in the writings gave any hints or suggestions, and John had no ideas of his own.

Wait a minute. Griffin wasn't only one man. What happened to his crew?

Some of the writing mentioned Griffin's team, but after a certain point, they were never mentioned again. John sat back, perplexed. Did they go back home? Did they grow old and die? What were they doing the last time they were mentioned?

He skimmed through the papers to find their last appearance and dropped them in shock.

The lead mine.

It was meant to be a future operation. How many men were in his crew? Thirteen, including Griffin.

Jessica said there were twelve casualties in the mining acci-dent. What the hell happened down there?

What did Jessica say? A mystery. Suspected gas leak. Signs of a struggle, minor injuries, but none life-threatening. From the notes, it was clear that Griffin's team had a strong sense of camaraderie. They trusted each other. Trusted him.

Zeluniel's comment about Griffin being a killer preyed on his mind.

This couldn't be true. John had clearly misunderstood. He had to have. He'd show her the papers in the morning. She was much smarter than him and would work out where he was going wrong. She'd set him straight. Griffin wasn't a murderer or a traitor. There was no way.

John put the thought aside and kept reading. The text blurred as he tried to put it all together. He found a passage about the siren call that he hadn't noticed before.

He sat bolt upright and read frantically, darting back and forth over the pages.

Griffin hadn't stuck around for so long because he wanted to protect Jessica. If he absorbed her soul, he would gain enough power to dominate or even banish the ethereals from the world.

John's head hurt. This was the opposite of what Griffin had told him to do. Save Jessica and keep her hidden. Do the right thing. What did Griffin think the right thing was? Was he hoping John would discover his papers after Jessica was rescued? Did he hope he'd follow through on the murderous plan to consume her essence? Or was this an idea long abandoned?

One line said, "Ought we delay the danger to mankind until another day or resolve the issue once and for all in the present?"

"Oh man," John muttered.

John read on. As time passed and Griffin's body and mind weakened with age, his willpower waned even with Yondarel's assistance. He questioned the mental fortitude and physical strength needed to fight the ethereals openly and the morality of the decision.

That must have been why he gave Yondarel to me and allowed himself to die.

John's chest ached with the pain of his friend's death, now

worsened by the knowledge that he wasn't the all-good and well-intentioned person he'd seemed. Griffin's serious contemplation of killing an innocent weighed heavily on John's mind. That it was Jessica made it worse. The ethereal was right: Griffin *was* a killer.

Anger built in John. His oldest and best friend had lied to him. He felt betrayed. Griffin had only been invested in acquiring power and either dominating or banishing the ethereals from the world. But was that a noble goal despite the horrifying act required? Maybe spiting the ethereals by snatching Jessica out of their grasp was just as important. He'd countered the ethereals for so long that denying them victory was just as, if not more, important as preventing the end of the world.

John realised he hadn't seen anything about ethereal victory ending the world. He frantically read through the bundles of paper again. Did he miss something? An explanation of how her death would end the world?

No. There was nothing.

"Son of a bitch!"

He had to share this with Jessica. It was too much for him alone.

He looked over where she slept.

It could wait until morning.

CHAPTER SIXTEEN

John yelled out and flailed his arms and legs to fight off a threat. His knees smashed against something: Griffin's desk. He was still in the shack.

John opened his eyes and looked around. Jessica still slept. She looked vulnerable; it would be so easy to break her ne—

He shook his head to interrupt the intrusive thought.

His brow dripped with sweat. A dream. Nightmare, perhaps. They were in a forest, he and the ethereals. He was surrounded, backed into a corner.

His face burned as he remembered his ghastly choice to defeat the ethereals.

He glared at the ring on his finger.

"Was that your doing?" he demanded.

The ring didn't reply.

The sensation was still so visceral, the taste of power lingering in his veins. Never again would he be powerless. Shaking his head, confusion clouded his thoughts. He would never hurt Jessica. Would he?

The fact that he had to ask alarmed him.

Her fear-stricken face as I put my hands around her throat ...

John stole a glance at Jessica. She looked uncomfortable, as if having a nightmare of her own. He stumbled to his feet and rushed outside.

It was still raining, but not as heavily as before. The car's interior was soaked. It was not going to be a pleasant drive when the sun rose.

He walked to the Griffin Tree Row, but Jessica's presence still tempted him.

John leaned against a tree and rolled a cigarette out of habit. He brought his lighter up, then stopped. Disgusted, he threw the cigarette on the ground. There was only one thing that could quench his need: Jessica. He had to stay away until he had complete control.

The rain came down most heavily. It filtered through the leaves above, and John let it wash over him. His clothes were soaked, but he couldn't get sick while Yondarel was with him.

Yondarel ...

He stared at the ring suspiciously.

Just how much influence did it have over him?

He wondered if Griffin's more horrifying thoughts and actions were truly his own.

Could John trust himself around Jessica under Yondarel's influence? She still needed his protection, but could he protect her from himself? He'd only had Yondarel one night, and they were already inextricably linked. He'd die from his injuries without it.

The door to the shack groaned open, and Jessica stepped out.

What is she thinking?! The sun hasn't risen. It's not time to go.

Her face was a mixture of terror and rage.

She had something in her hands.

Griffin's papers. Bundles of them.

Oh, fuck ...

"I heard you!" she screamed hoarsely.

"What?" John yelled. He pushed off the tree and walked towards her.

"Stay back!"

He stopped and held up his hands.

"I heard you talking before!" she screamed through the rain, her voice shrill.

"I don't know what you're talking about!"

"'Sorry, Jessica, this has to be done,' you said. I heard you!"

John's mind raced as he tried to recall when he could have said those words. His memory was a blur, but then a thought struck him—had he been talking in his sleep?

"How long were you planning this?" she asked, holding up the papers. Tears streamed down her face, mixed with the falling rain.

"I wasn't planning anything."

"I *heard* you!" she repeated hoarsely. She looked so defeated. So scared. So betrayed.

John took another step towards her.

"Stay back!" she screamed. Her voice broke.

How could he convince her of his intentions? Did he even know what his intentions were anymore?

"Please," he implored. "We can talk about this. Just get inside, out of the rain, where they can't find you."

She shook her head, eyes fiery with betrayal.

"I trusted you!"

"You still *can* trust me! But you need to get back inside before you draw them here."

"I saw what he wrote."

"I know it looks bad, but I can explain!"

Jessica's eyes darted around the open space; her body tensed as if ready to bolt. "I can't risk that. I can't risk my life that you're telling the truth."

John found himself at a loss. Negotiation was not his strong suit. Avoiding conversation whenever possible, he was more accustomed to being blunt and to the point. He had no persuasion skills to speak of. Jessica hadn't even trusted him when he first told her she was in danger.

Should he pick her up and carry her into the shack against her will? If he did, she'd never trust him again, but perhaps she wouldn't anyway. At least she'd be safe.

Or would she?

He didn't even know if he could trust himself anymore. He glared at Yondarel. It had caused this. It must have. Because of it, he'd had that dream, uttered those words Jessica had overheard. His uncertainty, his inability to trust himself around Jessica, it all traced back to Yondarel. Jessica wouldn't be reacting this way if not for its interference.

"Jessica, please, we can talk about this. Work it out."

"No," she said. "I don't know if I can trust you, and I know damned well I can't trust that thing on your finger."

She had a point. But still, he had to do something. He took another step.

"I said stay back!" she screamed in a high-pitched voice.

Jessica threw the papers on the wet ground. She took a cautious step to the side, edging away from him and the shack. Then another. John didn't move. He didn't want to scare her off.

Then she turned and splashed through the mud to the car.

"No, Jessica!" he yelled. "Don't do it! It's not safe!"

She screamed incoherently and started the engine. The wheels spun, and mud sprayed.

She gave him one final look of anger and betrayal before accelerating across the park, tearing up the muddy ground behind her.

He could still sense her presence and knew that the trust they'd established was lost forever.

John ran after her, but the car smashed over the kerb and onto the street. Something beneath the car scraped along the ground and sparked. The car fishtailed, tyres squealing before steadying and speeding away.

John couldn't keep up. He fell to his knees in the mud and the rain.

He'd failed her. He'd failed Griffin.

Jessica was gone, exposed and without protection. And there was nothing he could do about it.

CHAPTER SEVENTEEN

How did it all go wrong?

They had a plan. Wait until morning.

Why couldn't she wait?

They'd kill her, and it would be her own fault.

Not hers. It was Griffin's fault.

If he hadn't written down those stupid ideas, John wouldn't have had that nightmare and wouldn't have left the shack. Jessica wouldn't have found those papers, read them, and assumed the worst.

But those ideas weren't entirely Griffin's, were they?

Yondarel.

He glared at the cursed band of gold on his finger. If it hadn't put those poisonous ideas in Griffin's head, egged him on with ideas of domination and victory ... If it hadn't given John that nightmarish vision ...

No, it was my fault.

He could have spoken to Jessica about his fears instead of running outside in a panic. Could have had enough self-control to know he'd never harm her. Not have read Griffin's papers.

Not assaulted the stranger who only wanted to help Jessica. Any number of things could have led to a different outcome.

As it was, Jessica would be killed, and it was all John's fault.

He'd started the day with only one friend and had lost two in less than twenty-four hours. That had to be a world record.

John kneeled in the mud. The rain continued to ease. His head dropped, chin on his chest.

His only consolation was that the world wouldn't end. That was Griffin's lie to motivate him. But Jessica's world would end. She'd been running all night with him, had seen him grievously wound a man, kill several monsters, and possibly become addicted to their essence. And she was probably starving. He couldn't blame her.

Then John realised something.

Jessica hadn't gone towards the police station. She'd taken the road to the mountain.

She was without protection and trying to find a long-abandoned mine in the dark, all the while broadcasting her location to every ethereal in the world.

He could keep her safe even as she fled him if he followed her. He could steal another car. He didn't know how to drive, but he'd seen Jessica do it. Just put it in gear and put the clutch down, and … no. That wasn't an option.

Running would take at least an hour. He'd be far too late to help.

An idea struck him like a punch to the face.

The mud splashed as he jumped to his feet and raced up the street. If it was still there, he might just have a chance.

He arrived a minute later. The bike was still in the bike rack!

"Well, boys, look who's back again," came a voice behind him.

John spun around. There was Tom, a white medical dressing on his nose, and two of his idiots, all armed with bats. Rick, the broken-fisted, wasn't with them. It was probably the smartest thing he'd ever done.

Of course, they were here. They usually were before dawn. John hadn't even thought about them since Griffin had died.

"You owe us for earlier," Tom said with a sneer. "And the old man won't be quick enough to save you this time."

John groaned. He *really* didn't want to deal with this shit. There were real problems to solve.

"I'm only going to say this once," John said quietly. "You don't want to fuck with me right now."

Tom slapped his bat against his hand. "Tough words. Let's see what you've got to back them up."

They approached John, bats at the ready.

He sighed. Compared to the night he'd had, this was just pathetic.

Tom swung at him, but John grabbed the bat and effortlessly yanked it out of his hand. He swung the bat and knocked all three miscreants to the ground.

"Pathetic," he said. He *had* warned them.

He dropped the bat and walked to the bike rack, ignoring the moans and groans of the injured idiots.

John crouched and inspected the lock on the bike. He didn't have a bolt cutter, but he did have Yondarel's strength. He grabbed the chain and, with a swift, forceful jerk, snapped it. The sudden release of tension made the chain whip against the metal bike rack, which rang like a bell.

John slipped the snapped chain and lock into a pocket in his cargo pants and used the velcro to seal it. John was ready to hop on the bike when Tom stumbled towards him. He'd picked up the bat and was waving it around, screaming incoherently. Yondarel translated: he'd insulted John's parentage, sexuality, and skin colour.

John sighed and tried to go around him. Tom swung the bat, hitting him in the face.

Hurt him!

He dropped the bike and grabbed Tom by the throat, lifting

him off the ground and squeezing. Tom's eyes bulged, and the bat fell to the ground. He clawed at John's hands, but John was implacable. No more chances.

Kill!

He crushed the young man's throat, and his body went limp.

Consume!

John willed Tom's essence into himself. Brimming with power, he dropped the body like carelessly discarded rubbish.

He felt powerful.

Yondarel did too.

CHAPTER EIGHTEEN

John pedalled faster than ever along the quiet, tree-lined streets. Fortunately, the rain had stopped, and the full moon lay low on the horizon and peeked through the cloud cover, illuminating the pre-dawn darkness.

He turned right along the cemetery. There was activity within the grounds. Unusual for this time of day. He stopped the bike and took a closer look.

Bodies exhumed themselves from graves, controlled by ethereals. Many were naked or covered in shawls. Some well-established ethereals stood nearby, overseeing the efforts. No matter how skeletal or battered the bodies looked, a transformation occurred once the overseers approached them. It was hard to see from a distance, but John could sense that each body was given a ring, an anchor, and as the ethereal essence within made contact, the bodies began to regenerate. Muscles grew, skin formed, and in moments, they appeared fully alive. It was the same healing process that John experienced with Yondarel, albeit starting from a much more dire physical state.

He felt something else, a feeling he'd never encountered before.

Tunnels?

Not regular tunnels. Tunnels through reality.

Jessica's passage had clearly not gone unnoticed, and the ethereals were assembling an army.

He slammed his feet onto the pedals and rode as fast as possible. He needed to reach Jessica before this army did.

As John pedalled, he saw a morning jogger dragged into the bushes. Her screams abruptly cut off.

He felt sickened but couldn't do anything for her now. He had to reach Jessica.

When he rode past the bushes, the same woman walked out with a gold ring on her finger and an inhuman expression on her face.

As John continued, he witnessed more people caught by ethereals, killed, and reanimated as hosts. He had no idea how many new ethereals had entered the world this morning. The senseless murders seemed unreal to him, numbing him to them.

John rode beyond the residential areas to where the road narrowed. Before too long, the road cut directly through forestland. He could barely see through the trees and shrubs. The tall trees filtered what little moonlight broke through the clouds.

He turned right up the mountain, past empty picnic areas. His stamina was boundless. That was Yondarel's doing.

He turned left onto a muddy dirt road encroached by tall trees. The narrow path seemed to hold back the forest.

Fresh tyre marks in the mud confirmed what he already knew: Jessica had come this way. All along, he had been following the clarion call of her presence, which now beckoned from further up the mountain. He continued on.

Jessica's abandoned car lay on the path ahead, blocked by a downed tree. John rode around the obstacles, not even slowing to investigate. She wasn't in it. He could sense her presence further ahead.

He grimaced. She'd never find the mine's entrance without the car's headlights.

Rain bucketed down. John had been riding for half an hour. He hoped he wasn't too late.

He sensed both light and dark creatures ahead and rode as quickly as he could without slipping in the mud or crashing into a tree.

The ethereals had found her.

CHAPTER NINETEEN

John rode past a handful of ethereals fighting each other and squinted in the dim light.

A dark creature loomed before him, and John dodged. He swung his anchor-laden fist like a post-modern knight on horseback. It screamed and fell as its face burned.

He gripped the handlebars and continued through the undergrowth.

He didn't see the root, sending him flying off the bike. He landed hard on his chest but immediately jumped back to his feet. Yonderel would attend to the injury. He picked up the bike and swung it at a light creature approaching him. It roared and retreated.

Hefting the bike over his shoulder, John ran headlong into the dark forest towards Jessica's signal, tripping into a deep ditch. It annoyed him more than it hurt. As he clambered back to his feet, he noticed a tiny black cave on the side of the mountain. He moved closer.

A chain-link fence barred entry. Overgrown plant life covered faded warning signs. This was the abandoned mine. The place where Griffin had killed twelve of his friends and companions. John grabbed the fence and tore it apart.

He grabbed the bike and slung it back over his shoulder. It would do as a weapon against the light creatures since his ring was useless against them.

He could feel ethereal presences. Only a dozen had made it this high so far, but that would change once the reinforcements got up the path. He had to find Jessica quickly.

As John moved deeper into the forest, he focused on Jessica's siren call. It was like a beacon in the night, guiding him through the dense undergrowth. He had to reach her first.

John could hear the rustling of leaves, the snapping of twigs, and the distant echoes of ethereal movement. His heart pounded as he pushed forward, the urgency of the situation driving him on.

He found her.

She ran blindly headlong into the forest, away from the mine. On her heels were three ethereals: the dark creature Zhelktrakh and the light creatures Larulia and Unrelya. He called out to them. Unrelya turned to look at him, its glare blazing, but the others kept running.

He ran to Unrelya and smashed it in the face with the bicycle, again and again. It roared in anger, catching the bike in its hands and ripping it into pieces. Then he felt the presence of a starless night sky behind him and dodged.

Gralkrakh whipped past and slammed into Unrelya. They grappled and roared with inhuman voices. Unrelya tried to punch Gralkrakh with its anchor, but a bite to the wrist kept it back.

John left them to it and continued towards Jessica.

She had fallen and scrambled backwards, her back to a tree, seemingly resigned to her fate. Zhelktrakh—dark like a mine shaft—and Larulia—bright like an incandescent bulb—stalked towards her while trying to fend the other off.

John picked up a fallen branch and ran behind them, slamming it into Larulia's head. With a loud crack, her body flopped to the ground, neck twisted.

Zhelktrakh turned in surprise. John dropped the branch and leaped onto Zhelktrakh, pressing Yondarel into its face. It shrieked as it burned, batting him off and fleeing into the darkness of the forest.

John looked down at Jessica. She was soaked, dark hair matted to her face, his black leather jacket covered in mud and blood.

A gash bled down her cheek and another on her leg.

She looked at him with a mixture of relief and trepidation.

"I wasn't going to let them kill you." He extended his hand.

"You're insane. And awesome," she said quietly, pulling herself up.

Danger!

"Go!" John shouted. "That way!"

Jessica ran.

John turned to face a fully healed Larulia. He reached down to grab a large stick, but Larulia growled and punched him in the face. He responded with an uppercut. It contemptuously spat out a tooth. John feinted left, and Larulia moved to block him. He grabbed Larulia's outstretched arm and ripped the golden ring—Onsiyehr—off its finger. He threw it as far as he could into the forest.

Larulia screamed in rage and kicked him hard in the face before racing into the forest. John's nose broke, and he fell backward. But he didn't stay down. He jumped to his feet, his nose healing as he moved and plunged into the forest after it.

The forest was a dark, chaotic maze, the ground slick with mud and fallen leaves. Every step was treacherous. Low-hanging branches whipped at his face, and unseen roots threatened to trip him. But he didn't slow. He sensed Larulia's weakness, shorn of Onsiyehr, and he knew he had a chance to end it.

John's breath was loud, and his heart pounded, but he pushed himself harder, driven by a single-minded determination. He could hear Larulia crashing through the undergrowth ahead of him. He was gaining on it. He intended to end this, once and for all.

A strange sensation, like the one from the cemetery, lay ahead, mingling with Larulia's incandescent presence. But the ethereal was nowhere to be seen. Thinking it was a trick, he ran full speed and slipped out of the world.

CHAPTER TWENTY

John's senses were overwhelmed by the sheer intensity of the all-encompassing whiteness.

There was no forest. No darkness. No gravity.

Only white.

Rain droplets floated away from his body and into the white nothingness.

He stared into it, hypnotised. His quarry had escaped here.

The stark whiteness.

Like he had stepped into a pallid void, a complete absence of everything he knew.

The silence was so absolute, so profound that he could hear the sound of his own heartbeat, the rush of blood in his veins, the faint rustle of his clothes against his skin.

He could even hear the soft sound of his own breathing, the air rushing in and out of his lungs.

As the moments stretched on, he noticed the air thinning.

What little that accompanied him from the forest was slowly diffusing into the nothingness.

His lungs strained for breath, but he did not panic. He simply stopped breathing.

Yondarel kept him alive, healing him, sustaining him.

It was disorienting. The lack of sensory input made him feel as if he was floating in a sea of nothingness.

Time lost all meaning, minutes stretching into what felt like hours.

He had no idea how long he was there, only that he needed to find Jessica.

A dark spot in the corner of his eye, a minuscule difference in the homogenous environment, drew his attention.

He turned his head and beheld a gaping black void. A terrible maw of darkness that stretched out forever and overtook his senses. The blinding whiteness now only a memory.

Movement. Dark things moved in the darkness.

He was afraid.

His hand twitched.

Compelled to move.

It twitched again.

Was the ring trying to leave his hand?

He held onto it tightly.

Something dwelt within the golden object, a writhing circle of light that yearned to return to its own kind.

He turned back to the infinite brightness. Each side overwhelmed his senses. He closed his eyes.

A shift in the ethereal presences around him. Something had changed.

Movement. Light things moved in the white.

They were coming for him. Coming for Yondarel.

Dark things moved behind him.

They would tear him apart.

He flailed in a panic. Where was the tunnel?

They drew close.

He reached out with his senses. An echo of Jessica's presence somewhere close. He had to find his way back to her.

Was there an imperfection in the whiteness around him? The tunnel?

He couldn't move. There was no medium to move through.

Instead, he *willed* himself towards the imperfection.

The approaching armies of formless beings were almost upon him.

His mind felt for Jessica's presence. Yet, he remained still.

The opposing armies were upon him.

He tried one last time, and the light and the darkness collided behind him.

CHAPTER TWENTY-ONE

Rain. The smell of the forest. The sound of battle.

John opened his eyes. The tunnel had closed behind him. Why, he didn't know. But he was back in the world, and that's what mattered. He felt impossibly heavy after his weightless time in the other place.

The reinforcements had arrived. Countless melees occurred around him. John fought through the ranks of ethereals and darted through trees and undergrowth towards Jessica's presence.

It took some time, but he found her. She was surrounded and armed with a stick, but her strength was failing. The creatures had her backed against a rock wall and she could not retreat any farther.

The creatures knew they had her and advanced while fighting among themselves: light battling dark and dark battling light. Their lack of a united front was the only thing slowing them.

John launched himself with blinding speed and inhuman strength and slammed the ground, knocking the creatures off their feet. He made it to Jessica's side before the creatures could get back up.

"John!" she exclaimed with obvious relief.

John smiled, but he knew it was too late. There were too many to fight through and have Jessica survive the ordeal. He knew what needed to be done.

Kill.

"I'm so sorry, Jessica, but this is the only way."

Chapter Twenty-Two

Yondarel exulted. Its time had come.

Consume.

John leaned in towards Jessica and pressed his cigarette lighter into her hand. He whispered into her ear.

"No!" she cried.

John turned away from her and screamed a war cry. He barrelled into the ranks of the encroaching creatures. They parted, allowing him passage; he wasn't their target. As he passed the final row of creatures, he leaped high into the air.

"Jessica!" he yelled.

At the top of his jump, he slipped the ring off and, with an inhuman roar, hurled Yondarel at her as hard as he could.

The assembled ethereals turned at his roar and impotently watched the anchor fly over their heads like a golden missile.

Jessica caught the ring, the force of its impact slamming her against the wall.

John landed, aghast. Had he killed her?

A blast erupted from Jessica, knocking the creatures to the ground.

She punched the ground, further disorienting the gathered

masses. She stood tall and ran through their ranks with startling speed.

John laughed maniacally.

She glanced back at John with an expression at once grateful and mournful. The gash on her face and the cut on her leg were gone. With a swish of John's leather jacket, she disappeared into the forest.

Without the ring, John could no longer feel the dark and light presences. He moved to block them from chasing Jessica and reached into his cargo pants pocket. He pulled out the bike chain with the lock still attached. It felt heavy without Yondarel augmenting his strength. He panted. He didn't have the same stamina either.

His bruises returned. The ethereals, in their stolen human forms, swarmed towards him, swiping at each other as they did. John rocked back and forth impatiently while waiting for the first to reach him. He swung the chain and smashed the padlock into the ethereal's face. It roared as blood spurted from its human nose.

He belted another ethereal in the kneecap, forcing its human body to the ground.

His eyebrow split open, and he winced. He stomped on the fallen ethereal's head, but without Yondarel's help, it didn't do much. The ethereal roared and kicked up at John, striking with surprising force, knocking him onto his back. The chain slipped from his grip. He slid and fell down an embankment, sticks and rocks cutting him as he tumbled down.

His lip spontaneously split open, and blood streamed down his chin.

John staggered back to his feet. From his lower vantage point, he saw that Jessica had reached the mine. The ethereals swarmed after her, but the crest of the rise shielded her from their view. It would only be seconds until they climbed the rise and realised what she was doing. She needed more time.

He limped and clambered up the embankment, yelling incoherently at the ethereals. His head was cloudy. His eyes itched. His shoulders hunched, and he put his hands on his knees, winded.

His arms and neck opened as if cut by an invisible knife.

"Come back!" he screamed. "I killed Nashgrakh. I ran him over with a fucking train! Fight me!"

Pain in his neck like whiplash. Bruises spread across his back.

He limped on. Some turned to look. Others fought to reach Jessica first.

John's shoulder dislocated, and he cried out in pain.

"I killed Zeluniel! I broke her fucking neck and ate her soul!"

His forearm snapped, and he screamed.

"I'm responsible for Yekhtreshk's death! I softened him up so he could be killed!"

The creatures were now far in the distance.

He couldn't yell anymore. His throat constricted and bruised. He limped on vainly until his ankle broke, and he fell.

Jessica was beyond his help now. He'd done all he could.

John squinted into the distance and caught one final glance of her as she crawled into the entrance of the mine.

Keep going, Jessica, just a little farther ...

Scrapes and cuts opened on John's face as he crawled along the forest floor.

He looked again at the ethereals crowded around the mine's entrance. Something had changed.

They weren't moving.

He clawed his way across the muddy ground towards them. His shoulder bones shattered, and he cried out hoarsely, his throat ruined.

The ethereals seemed confused. Had the lead mine so effectively blocked her presence that they couldn't sense her anymore? Did they think she had tunnelled out of the world like they could? Without Yondarel to enhance his understanding, he could only guess.

Suddenly, the ethereals resumed their fight. But it had a different tenor now their target had vanished: orgiastic spasms of heightened violence, panic, and desperation.

John's fists re-broke, and the ethereals continued to fight.

He watched with detached interest. His participation was at an end. He might as well enjoy the show.

More scrapes and bruises blossomed across his broken body.

The ethereal forces, John guessed, were committed to the battle. Retreat, they must have thought, would result in a rout. Without Yondarel's supplementary information, he was left in the dark. His thoughts turned to Jessica, silently wishing for her safety. Whispered directions to the mine entrance and his lighter were the only aid he could offer her. The hope that it would lighten her path was his only comfort; he had no idea what would come next.

His left arm ripped and detached, splashing into the mud. Blood gushed out, and he vomited in pain.

He tried to distract himself with the battle.

It seemed as hopeless as the ones he'd read about in Griffin's journals, but this time none of them had the home-ground advantage. It was a fight to the death.

Good riddance.

What was a desperate final battle for Jessica's essence had instead become a spasm of violence and fear. They must have assumed she was gone forever, and all was lost.

His right arm tore off. John screamed. Blood drenched his clothes and pooled beneath him, mixed with the mud. He didn't have much time.

All at once, the bodies controlled by the ethereals collapsed like marionettes without strings. Some exploded into clouds of dust and steam like Griffin had. Others seemed to rot as they fell, and a few looked like they had merely fallen asleep.

They must have retreated to their ethereal realms.

Dawn's light appeared and bathed the tops of the trees high above him. The darkness of night was banished. The sunlight hadn't yet touched him, but he felt comforted, nonetheless.

He collapsed onto his back and allowed himself to fall apart, to finally feel Griffin's death. This wasn't how things should have gone. He cried and sobbed like a child, tears mixing with the rain, their release like the cleansing of a wound.

It wasn't fair.

He felt himself fade. He'd lost so much blood.

At least Jessica had made it. He mightn't have saved the world, but he had saved her, and that was one thing he could be proud of.

John hoped she'd remember him for the good he'd tried to do. He hoped she was safe.

Lying on the forest floor, he remembered his dream of living out his days in the wilderness, free from everything.

Rain sprinkled his face. The storm would soon pass.

He breathed out and relaxed and joined the darkness.

Reader,

You've shared John's path to the end of this tale. Now, I ask you to take one more step.

Share this story.

There are other readers out there waiting for a tale like this. Your words, especially a review or a mention, can be a beacon in the dark, guiding them to these pages.

Why? Because stories aren't meant to be hoarded like treasures in a locked vault. They're meant to be passed on, from one hand to another, from one mind to another. Your voice can make this book live, breathe, and thrive in places I can't reach.

So, if you found something in these pages that stirred you, that made you think or feel, consider telling someone about it. Let this story live in more minds.

Thank you for your support.

With gratitude,

D.P. Vaughan

P.S. The ethereal infestance is not over. It's brewing, like a storm on the horizon. Stay tuned, and don't get too comfortable. The ride's not over yet.

Acknowledgments

Editors
Rebecca Brewer
Adam vanLangenberg
at Fireside Editing firesideediting.com.au

Designers
Cover art by Miblart miblart.com
Dinkus designed by Irha Graphics

Consultants
Jayla Jacobs
Asher Gilbertson
Neff Rodriguez

Vietnamese translator
Toan Le

Music
Vindsvept youtube.com/@Vindsvept

To stay up to date, and receive other free short stories, sign up to D.P. Vaughan's newsletter at dpvaughan.com.

ABOUT THE AUTHOR

D.P. Vaughan is an Australian author who writes speculative fiction thrillers for adult readers. Her works focus on marginalised people.

She grew up in Townsville, and moved to Brisbane to study music composition and later earned her master's degree as a specialist English teacher.

She has an avid interest in history, science and linguistics, and lives with her children in a quiet suburb of Canberra where she teaches English to adult migrants, refugees, and asylum seekers.